THE PENTAGON'S "CENTER 18"

DEEP INSIDE THE REMOTE FORESTS
OF THE PACIFIC NORTHWEST,
A GROTESQUE ROTTING MANSION
STANDS ALONE, ITS SMILING
GARGOYLES SILHOUETTED AGAINST
THE THICK, OMINOUS SILENCE.

MARINE SENTRIES GUARD IT

WITHIN ITS WALLS ECHO THE
MUFFLED CRIES OF TWENTY-SEVEN
MEN WHO—FOR NO APPARENT REASON
—HAVE GONE TOTALLY MAD.

THE
NINTH
CONFIGURATION

WILLIAM PETER BLATTY

BANTAM BOOKS · TORONTO · NEW YORK · LONDON

THE NINTH CONFIGURATION
A Bantam Book

PRINTING HISTORY
Harper & Row edition published August 1978
2nd printing .... August 1978
Bantam edition / February 1980

ISBN 0-553-13353-5

Published simultaneously in the United States and Canada

*Bantam Books are published by Bantam Books, Inc. Its trade-
mark, consisting of the words "Bantam Book" and the por-
trayal of a bantam, is Registered in U.S. Patent and Trademark
Office and in other countries. Marca Registrada. Bantam
Books, Inc., 666 Fifth Avenue, New York, New York 10019.*

PRINTED IN THE UNITED STATES OF AMERICA

For the purposes of this story, I have taken some liberties with the facts; there are, for example, neither psychiatrists nor medical officers in the United States Marine Corps.

—WPB

For Linda

Author's Note

When I was young and worked very hastily and from need, I wrote a novel called *Twinkle, Twinkle, Killer Kane!* Its basic concept was surely the best I have ever created, but what was published was just as surely no more than the notes for a novel—some sketches, unformed, unfinished, lacking even a plot.

But the idea mattered to me, so once again I have written a novel based on it. This time I know it is the best that I can do.

"I have some rights of memory
in this kingdom . . ."
Hamlet, V, 2

THE
NINTH
CONFIGURATION

The mansion was isolated and Gothic, massive, trapped in a wood, grotesque. It crouched beneath the stars under clustered spires like something enormous and deformed, unable to hide, wanting to sin. Its gargoyles grinned at the forest pressing in on it thickly all around. For a time nothing moved. Dawn sifted in. Thin fall sunlight pried at the morning entombed within the arborescent gloom, and fog curled up from rotted leaves like departing souls, dry and weak. In the breeze, a creaking shutter moaned for Duncan and a haunted crow coughed hoarsely in a meadow far away. Then silence. Waiting.

The voice of a man from within the mansion carried with firm conviction, startling a small green heron from the moat.

"Robert Browing had the clap and he caught it from Charlotte and Emily Brontë."

A second man, angry, bellowed, "Cutshaw, shut your mouth!"

"He caught it from *both* of them."

"Shut up, you crazy bastard!"

"You don't want to hear the truth."

"Krebs, sound Assembly!" the angry man ordered.

Then a military bugling shattered the air, ripping into the fog, and an American flag, fluttering defiance, leaped up a pole atop a spire. Twenty-seven men in green fatigues exploded like shrapnel from the mansion and hurtled out to the center of its courtyard, muttering and mumbling and crooking their elbows, dress-right-dress, in the forming of a military line. Above their denims some affected other dress: one wore a rapier and golden earrings; from the head of another bloomed a coonskin cap. Imprecations floated up from them like steam alive with sparks:

"Hillo ho ho, boys! Come, bird, come!"

"You know, I wish you'd douche; sincerely."

"Sink the *Bismarck!*"

"Watch the elbow!"

A man with a shaggy mongrel dog in his arms burst into the center of the line. He bawled, "My cape! Have you seen my cape?"

"Hell, what's a cape?" snarled the one with the sword. "Just fucking fabric."

"Fabric?"

"Foolish fucking fabric."

"What country is this?" asked a man at the end of the line.

A blond-haired man confronted them briskly. He wore tattered and dirty black Keds, his left great toe protruding through a hole; and over his fatigues he flaunted a New York University sweater: on the sleeve of one arm were letterman's stripes, and on the other, a NASA astronaunt's patch. "Attention!" he commanded with authority. "It is I: Billy Cutshaw!"

The men obeyed, then stiffly raised their arms in the salute of ancient Rome. "Captain Billy, let us serve you!" they howled into the fog; then they dropped their arms and stood unmoving, hushed, like the damned awaiting judgment.

Cutshaw's gaze flicked over them swiftly, flashing and mysterious, luminous and deep. At last he spoke:

"Lieutenant Bennish!"

"Sah!"

"You may take three giant steps and kiss the hem of my garment!"

"*Sah!*"

"The *hem,* Bennish, mind you, the *hem!*"

Bennish took three steps forward, then cracked his heels together resoundingly. Cutshaw measured him with reserve. "Excellent form, Bennish."

"Thank you very much, sir."

"Don't let it go to your fucking head. There is nothing more vile than *hubris.*"

"Yes, sir. You've said that many times, sir."

"I know that, Bennish." Cutshaw was probing him with his gaze as though seeking out insolence and outrage, when the man with the sword bawled, "Here comes the fuzz!"

The men began booing as out from the mansion, in angry stride, marched the starched and militant figure of a major in the Marine Corps. Cutshaw scuttled into the line, and over the booing the man with the sword shouted out at the major, "Where's my Ho Chi Minh decoder ring? I sent in the goddam boxtops, Groper; where the hell's the—"

"*Quiet!*" Gordon quelled them. His little eyes seared out from a face that was pummeled beef adorned with a crew cut. He was hulking and heavy of bone. "Fucking weirdo yellow smartass college pricks!" he snarled.

"*That* says it," muttered someone in the ranks.

Groper paced the rank of men, his great head lowered as though ready to charge them. "Who in the hell do you think you're kidding with your phony little squirrel act? Well, bad news, boys. Tough shit. 'Cause guess who's coming to take command next week! Can you guess, boys? Huh? A *psychiatrist!*" He was suddenly roaring, quivering with uncontrollable rage. "That's right! The best! The best in uniform! The greatest fucking psychiatrist since Jung!" He pronounced the *J.*

Now he stood breathing heavily, gathering air and dominion. "Fucking combat-shirking bastards! He's coming to find out if you're really psycho!" Groper grinned, his eyes shining. "Isn't that great news, boys?"

Cutshaw took one step forward. "Could we knock off this 'boys' shit, Major, please? It makes us feel like we're cocker spaniels and you're the Old Pirate in *Tortilla Flat*. Could we—"

"*Back into line!*"

Cutshaw squeezed a rubber horn in his hand the size of a baseball. It emitted a raucous, unpleasant sound.

Groper rasped, "Cutshaw, what have you got there?"

"A foghorn," answered Cutshaw. "Chinese junks have been reported in the area."

"Someday I'll break your back, I promise you."

"Someday I'm going to leave Fort Zinderneuf; I'm getting tired of propping up bodies."

"I wish they'd clobbered you in space," said Groper.

The men began to hiss.

"Quiet!" barked Groper.

The hissing grew louder.

"Yeah, hissing you're good at, you slimy little snakes."

"Bra-*vo!* Bra-*vo!*" commended Cutshaw, leading the men in polite applause. Others added their praise:

"Good image."

"Splendid, Groper! Splendid!"

"Just one more thing, sir," Cutshaw began.

"What's that?"

"Stick a pineapple up your ass." Cutshaw looked away. He felt a premonition. "Somebody's coming," he said.

It was a prayer.

The trouble had begun with Nammack. On May 11, 1967, Nammack, a captain in the United States Air Force, was piloting a B-52 on a bombing run headed for Hanoi when his co-pilot reported hydraulic malfunction, whereupon Nammack had quietly stood up, slipped off his high-altitude flying helmet and said softly and confidently, "This looks like a job for Superman."

The co-pilot took control. Nammack was hospitalized and persisted in his delusion that he had superhuman powers and could not be totally cured "without Kryptonite." Yet psychiatric testing and evaluation yielded the tantalizing conclusion that Nammack could not clearly be labeled psychotic. Up until the moment he had stood up in the cockpit, in fact, all the evidence suggested that his psyche and emotions were remarkably sturdy.

Nammack was the forerunner. Soon he was followed by dozens, then scores: military officers manifesting sudden mental disturbance, usually involving some form of obsession that was striking and bizarre. In no case was there any history of mental or emotional imbalance.

Government authorities were baffled and grew increasingly disturbed. Were the men malingerers? It was noted that the Nammack case had occurred very shortly after Captain Brian Fay, a Marine who had refused to enter a combat zone, was sentenced to years of hard labor. The war was controversial, and most of the men involved were in combat or scheduled for combat. The suspicion that their illness was feigned was inevitable.

But there were problems with such a conclusion. Some of the men were not involved in a combat-related situation; and many of those who were had been decorated for valor. Why were all of them officers? Why did most cases involve an obsession? The darker suspicion of a White House staff paper on the subject suggested an underground cult of officers whose purposes were unknown but potentially dangerous. In the face of the enigma, it was not hard to entertain such ideas.

To probe the mystery, and—if indicated—to seek its cause and cure, the government established Project Freud, a secret network of military rest camps where the men were hidden from the public and studied. The last of these camps was Center Eighteen. Highly experimental in nature, it was based in a mansion deep in a forest of spruce and pine trees near the seacoast of Washington State. Built to match the medieval-castle home of her German husband, the Count of Eltz, the mansion belonged to Amy Biltmore, who had abandoned it long before she loaned it to the military in the fall of 1968. Now it was occupied by a skeleton staff of Marines and twenty-seven inmates, all of them officers: some Marine Corps; others former crewmen of B-52s; and one former astronaut, Captain Billy Thomas Cutshaw, who had aborted a mission to the moon during final countdown in a manner so extraordinary that only those present believed it.

To Cutshaw and the others at Center Eighteen the

Pentagon assigned a brilliant Marine Corps psychiatrist noted for his singular open-mindedness and astonishing success with often novel methods, Colonel Hudson Stephen Kane. Someone answering to that name did appear at the center on March 17, just a few weeks after the recapture of Hué. Major Groper, the adjutant at the center and temporarily in command, was confronting the inmates in the courtyard at the time, and when he observed the approach of the staff car whose occupant he guessed must be Colonel Kane, he cursed his fate that it should arrive during morning formation, when the inmates were always at their worst. Like feverish lice they had raced to the center of the mansion courtyard—all but Fairbanks, the one with the fencing foil, who had rummaged through his options that morning and elected to swing down to formation on a rope that he had fastened to a mansion spire. Now they were playing a game invented by Cutshaw called Speaking in Tongues, each man babbling cryptic madness at the top of his voice, except for Reno, the inmate with the dog. Reno stared straight ahead in a daze while singing "Let Me Entertain You." His dog looked frightened by the alien shouting.

"Oh, Christ!" Groper spat at the dust at his feet and then roared, "Attention! Shut up, you cocksuckers! Shut the hell up and fall in! *Fall in!*"

The inmates ignored him.

The staff car halted by the mansion entrance. The sergeant driver opened the door for the man in the back, a Marine Corps colonel who emerged and stood silently, watching Groper and the inmates. The colonel was tall and huskily built, his features rugged yet somehow gentle. Only in his eyes was there any movement: greenish flecks subtly spinning in pools of chestnut brown. There was sadness in them.

"Gentlemen, may I have your attention for a moment?" Groper's gravelly voice was unctuous.

The inmates continued with their game. The colonel watched them, his face unreadable, then he turned his head to the side. Next to him, in the neatly pressed gabardine shirt and pants of a class B uniform, stood a somber Marine with medic's insignia and colonel's leaves on his collar. In his hand he gripped a stethoscope. He was staring at the inmates and shaking his head. "Poor bastards," he muttered. Then he looked at the colonel. "Kane?"

The colonel acknowledged with a nod.

"I'm Colonel Fromme, the center medic. Sure glad you're aboard. I can use all the help I can possibly get." He looked at the inmates, who once again were out of control. "Jesus, they're really far gone."

"Would you please direct me to my quarters?" asked Kane.

"Just follow the yellow brick road."

Kane stared.

"Lieutenant Fromme, *fall in!*" roared Groper. He was looking at the man with the stethoscope.

"Fromme, you maniac!" came a shout from a trouserless man striding out from the mansion's front door. "Give me back my pants and stethoscope, dammit!" He stomped toward Kane and Fromme.

A deadpan sergeant, crisply uniformed, popped to attention in front of Kane and saluted smartly. "Sergeant Christian reporting for duty, sir!"

"And blasted well about *time,* Kildare!" Fromme greeted the sergeant icily. He pointed a finger at Kane. "God bless it, will you get this man into surgery or do you plan to let him stand here bleeding to death while you and your buddies play soldier! What the hell is this, for Chrissakes, a hospital or a nuthouse?"

Even as Fromme was finishing, Sergeant Christian was escorting him away forcibly. Meantime, the man with no pants arrived, and passing Fromme, deftly ripped away the stethoscope as he shouted at Sergeant Christian, "This time don't let him wrinkle the pants!" Then he turned to Kane and saluted.

An odd expression passed briefly across Kane's face and the man uttered, "Vincent!"

Kane sank into his former inscrutability. "What did you say?" he asked.

"You look exactly like Vincent van Gogh. Either that or a lark in a wheat field; I'm not sure which. It's pretty close. I'm Colonel Richard Fell. I'm the medic."

Kane studied him. A thickset man in his middle forties with sly, merry eyes in a downcast face, he was weaving slightly and the hand that he held in salute was the one that gripped the stethoscope.

"Colonel Fell, have you been drinking?" Kane's voice was soft and gentle, void of any semblance of accusation.

"What? In uniform?" Fell glared. "That's my last pair of gabardine pants he's got," Fell explained. "All the others are out at the cleaners, and, Colonel, if you're planning on my holding this salute much longer, would you please call Memorial Hospital and tell them that the donor arm is ready for the transplant? I expect it to be falling off almost any—"

Kane returned his salute.

"Thank you. You're a prince of the realm, sir, I swear it."

Another sergeant, heavily freckled, appeared before Kane and popped a salute. "Sergeant Krebs reporting for duty, sir."

"Would you show me to my quarters?"

Fell belched and murmured, "Probably," his eyes averted. Then, unaccountably, he turned and left them.

For a moment Kane watched him. Then he followed Krebs, who led him past the inmates toward the entrance of the mansion.

The inmates continued to babble. Groper implored them to come to attention. He'd been passed over twice for promotion; only a rating of "outstanding" on his next efficiency report could possibly save him from burial at his present rank. He glared at the inmates. "For Chrissakes, *quiet!*" he bawled.

"Groper, you have to say 'Simon says'!" instructed Cutshaw.

Groper roared, "Simon says, 'Attention!' "

The men instantly came to attention and fell to silence, all but the one with the earrings and the sword, who commenced to read Groper his rights: "You have the right to remain silent," he began to drone.

Kane's appraisal brushed over each man in the group. Then his gaze locked on the blue, unblinking eyes of Billy Cutshaw, staring intently into his own.

Kane returned Groper's salute and walked on to the mansion doorway. There he turned. Captain Cutshaw's eyes were still on him. Kane's large and sinewy fingers gently brushed along his face, tracing a memory, an ugliness, that a Korean plastic surgeon had effaced for him years ago: a scar that had jagged like lightning from his eye to the base of his jaw.

He went inside.

Later, Groper brooded in his office, declining from a rage to a dismal sulk. The eleventh most decorated American serviceman in World War II, many times commended for valor in Korea, he had risen through the ranks, beginning with a battlefield commission during the Battle of the Bulge. His career had held a promise now worn and faded and unfulfilled; and his personal life was a litter of rejections. Nothing within him had grown except anger. Now he hated the inmates. And Kane, before whom he had been humiliated.

Kane. There was something odd about him, thought Groper. He could not exactly put his finger on it. It was something out of place; yet familiar.

It made him uneasy.

3

Fell's clinic reeked of defiance. On the walls, in heavy crayon, bold red arrows pointed to jars containing "Aspirin," "Band-Aids," "Dental Floss" and "Lemon Drops." Another pointed out a "Suggestion Box"; and above them all, a master inscription, crayoned in green, proclaimed: "SELF-SERVICE."

Fell was standing by a skeleton that was hanging next to his desk. He tipped a bottle of Scotch that he had set in the base of the skull so that its contents poured through a space where some teeth were missing and into the coffee mug he was holding underneath the mouth of the bottle. "Don't blame *me*," he muttered. "I *told* them not to operate." He sipped at the Scotch and coffee and grimaced; then he picked up a stack of folders from his desk and stepped out into the great main hall of the mansion.

Like the exterior, the hall was a mixture of Tudor and Gothic, massive and dense, with stone-block walls and a high cathedral ceiling crisscrossed by beams. Circling the hall were a number of rooms now used as the commanding officer's office, the adjutant's office, the clinic, a utility room and a dormitory for the inmates. Plastered against one wall of the enormous area was a blowup of a poster for the motion picture *Dracula;* the copy read: "Bloody Terror of Transylvania." At the opposite end, a winding staircase led upstairs to a second floor, where the staff was billeted. The hub of the main hall below was used as a therapy room for the inmates. It was cluttered with lounge chairs, chess sets, Ping-Pong tables, stereo, a motion picture screen and projectors; coffee and soft-drink and cigarette machines; writing tables and magazines; and canvases, set on easels, vivid with paintings by the inmates. No painting was quite completed. Each was a tale of horror abruptly halted in mid-narration. One showed an index finger that pointed straight up and was pierced by a needle, dripping blood. Another depicted a tree, its terminal branches metamorphosed into the coils of a boa constrictor crushing the head of a male infant; its creator had captioned it "Mother Love." Still others were infinitely busy and chaotically detailed, yet executed with fine-drawn precision so that in a single painting one could identify a jackhammer, part of an arm and an onrushing train, the wheels of a lathe, a baleful eye, a Negro Christ, a bloody ax, a bullet in flight and a creature half-lizard, half-man. One painting depicted a city in flames, erupting clouds of thick black smoke, while above the scene, high, almost microscopic in size, hung a silvery bomber pierced by a spear; on the fuselage, in red, were the tiny letters ME.

Fell glanced around the hall. It was strangely quiet and deserted. He walked to Kane's office, opened the door and stepped inside.

Kane was unpacking some books from a large valise on his desk. His back was to Fell, but as the door slid open silently, he turned with a graceful swiftness.

"How're you doing?" asked Fell. He closed the door behind him.

"Do you plan to get dressed?" Kane asked him. Fell was still trouserless.

"How the hell can I get dressed when Lieutenant Fromme won't surrender my pants?" he answered. "You don't want me to *rip* them off!"

"No, we mustn't be repressive," said Kane.

"We mustn't wrinkle the pants!"

"Of course." Kane's voice was gentle, as though everything living were his patient. He took more books from the suitcase on the teakwood desk and moved toward some bookshelves in a wall on which an American flag now rested at a diagonal where once hung a medieval lance. The room had been a den. It was heavily paneled in a rich dark oak, and stuffed animal trophies brooded on high. Only the flag announced a present time; that, and on the wall behind the desk, photos of President Lyndon Johnson and the Chairman of the Joint Chiefs of Staff, in matching frames and posed in attitudes suggesting that the two were no longer speaking.

"Here," said Fell as he tossed the folders onto the desk. "Here's a present for you: case histories of the men."

Fell's eye fell inadvertently on a book in Kane's valise. It was a Roman Catholic missal. For the briefest instant he pondered its implications; then he looked up again at Kane.

"May I give you some advice?" said Fell.

The office door flew open, banging against the wall with a crash that loosened plaster from the ceiling. "Can I come in?" asked Cutshaw, the astronaut. He slammed the door behind him and marched toward Kane. "I'm Billy Cutshaw," he announced with menace. "So you're the new boy."

Kane finished shelving some books and turned. "Yes, I'm Colonel Hudson Kane."

"Do I call you Hud?"

"Why not call me Colonel?"

"Are you the one that makes the chicken?"

"Colonel Kane's a psychiatrist," offered Fell, flopping down on the seat of a large bay window.

"Sure. And they told me you were a doctor," Cutshaw rebutted. He pointed at Fell: "This man treats crocodiles for acne. Listen, pack up and leave, Hud! I don't give a shit if you're Shirley MacLaine! I am acting on orders to inform you that you're on the way out! Get moving! Get your ass into gear!" He knocked Kane's suitcase off the desk.

Kane stared calmly. "Someone 'ordered' you?" he asked. *"Who* ordered you, Cutshaw?"

"Unseen forces far too numerous to enumerate. Check the file; it's all in the file!" Cutshaw had seized the dossiers on the desk and was rapidly scanning the names on their covers, tossing one folder and then another on the floor. "It's all in the file," he announced excitedly, "under the heading 'Mysterious Voices.' Joan of Arc was *not* demented; she had acutely sensitive hearing!" Cutshaw threw away all the folders but one. "Hah! Here it is! My file! This is it! Here, read it, Hud. Read it out loud. It's my therapy."

"Why don't we—"

"Read it or I'll go crazy, dammit! I swear it! And *you'll be responsible!"*

"All right, Cutshaw." Kane took the folder from the astronaut's hand. "Sit down."

Cutshaw swooped to Fell and sat on his lap. Something crunched. Cutshaw said, "I think the end of the world just came for that bag of Fritos in my pocket."

Fell continued looking into his coffee mug, his expression unchanged. "Would you please tell Fromme I'd like my pants," he said to the astronaut.

" 'Consider the lilies of the field.' "

Then Cutshaw leaped up from Fell's lap and glided to a straight-backed wooden chair by the desk. He stared up unblinkingly at Kane. "I'm waiting," he told him.

Kane began to read: "Cutshaw, Billy Thomas, Captain, United States Marine Corps. . . ."

Cutshaw silently formed the words with his lips as Kane continued to read aloud:

". . . Two days prior to a scheduled space shot, subject officer, while dining on the base, was observed to pick up a plastic catsup bottle, squeeze a thin red line across his throat, and then stagger and fall heavily across a table then occupied by the director of the National Space Administration, gurgling, 'Don't—order—the swordfish.' "

There ensued a silence of several seconds. Kane's eyes were fixed on the file. Fell picked lint from his shirt.

Cutshaw's hand flew up to a medal that hung from his neck. "You're looking at my medal!" he snapped at Kane. "Stop looking at my medal!"

"I'm not."

"Yes, you are! You covet it!"

Kane looked down at the file. Once more he began to read. "On the following—"

"Isn't it beautiful?"

"Yes, it's—"

"Son of a bitch! I *knew* it. You were looking at it!"

"Sorry."

"Sure, you're sorry! What good is 'sorry'? The damage is done, you envious swine! How can I *eat* now, how can I *sleep!* I'll be a quivering nervous wreck now, waiting for some covetous kleptomaniacal colonel to come padding up to my bedside and rip away my medal!"

"If I were to do that," Kane said soothingly, "you would awaken."

"Powerful drugs could be insinuated into my soup."

Kane's eyes brushed over him, then returned to the dossier.

"The following morning at 0500, subject officer entered his space capsule, but on receiving instruction from Control to begin his countdown, he was heard instead to say, 'I am sick unto death of being used!' While being carried out of the capsule, subject officer plainly announced that if 'nominated' he 'would not run, and if elected would spend his term in office vomiting.' He later expressed his 'profound conviction' that going to the moon was 'naughty, uncouth, and in any case bad for his skin.' "

Fell's effort to suppress a giggle attracted a furious glance from Cutshaw. "What's the matter? You think that's funny?" Cutshaw bolted from his chair and began plucking books from the shelves and tossing them to the floor. "Pack up and leave, Hud! I've had it!"

He broke off and stared at the cover of a book in his hand. "What the hell is this: Teilhard de Chardin?" He looked with surprise at other titles on the shelf. "Douay Bible, Thomas à—" Cutshaw shook his head, then walked over to Kane. "Show me a Catholic and I'll show you a junkie," he said; then he ripped the psychiatrist's shirtsleeve from the wrist all the way to the shoulder and scrutinized his arm. Finally he turned to Fell and scowled. "His needle holes are cleverly hidden," he accused.

Kane said quietly, "Why won't you go to the moon?"

"Why do camels have humps and cobras none? Good Christ, man, don't ask the heart for reasons! Reasons are dangerous! The truth of the matter is Custer called Sitting Bull a Spic. Now, aren't you glad you found that out?"

"Why won't you go?" persisted Kane.

"Why should I? What the hell's up there?"

"When Christopher Columbus sailed from Spain, did he ever dream that he'd find America?"

"All he ever dreamed about was compasses. Idiot starts out looking for India and then plants the flag on Pismo Beach."

"It's—"

"Hud, I've *seen* the moon rocks! They've got little bits of glass inside them: isn't that exciting?"

"You still haven't given me a reason, Cutshaw."

"Only schmucks dance after dinner," Cutshaw intoned. "Sheiks sleep."

"What does that mean?" asked Kane.

"How do *I* know?" yipped Cutshaw defensively. "The *voices* told me to say that!"

"Cutshaw—"

"Wait a minute, wait wait wait!" The astronaut sat in the chair again as his hand flew up to his brow. His eyes pressed tightly shut in thought. "I'm getting a message from the astral plane. It's Attila the Hun. He wants to know if you'll accept the charges."

"No," said Fell.

"You tell him!"

The door flew open.

"Dr. Fell, I need attention."

An inmate in a beret stood framed in the doorway. In one hand he held a palette, in the other a brush.

"What's the problem?" Fell asked.

"Who but Leslie! Always Leslie!"

"Captain Leslie Morris Fairbanks," Fell told Kane.

The beret quivered with outrage. "Once *again* he has given me that fiendish Mark of Fairbanks! Look!" He pointed, turning. "I am bleeding!"

He wasn't. But slashed into his trouser seat was a very visible *F*.

"Is this wound self-inflicted?" asked Fell.

But the inmate was eying Kane. "You are Colonel Kane?"

Kane nodded.

"Charmed. I am Michelangelo Gomez." Gomez rubbed his paintbrush into the palette. "Your coloring is bilious," he said.

"Look out!" cried Fell; but too late: in a lightning movement, Gomez had brushed red paint onto both Kane's cheeks.

"There!" Gomez beamed. "Not a Protrait of Jenny, but at least no more Dorian Gray!" He raised his paintbrush high in salute. *"Ciao!"* he said, and left.

Kane heard heavy breathing. Cutshaw was standing inches away, his eyes staring madly, shining and wide. "Okay, now I'm ready for my ink-blot test," he said. He swooped to the chair, dragged it over to the desk, sat down, and looked expectant. "Come on, let's go."

"You want an ink-blot test?" asked Kane.

"What the hell, am I talking to myself? I want it

now while you're fresh with all those roses in your cheeks."

Kane wiped his face with a handkerchief. "We have no Rorschach cards."

"Like hell. Take a look in the drawer," Cutshaw told him.

Kane pulled the desk drawer open and removed a stack of Rorschach cards. "Very well," he said, sliding into the chair behind the desk. "Sit down."

Fell ambled toward the desk to observe.

Kane held a Rorschach card up and the astronaut leaned his head in close, his eyes scrunched up in concentration as he studied the ink blot.

"What do you see?" asked Kane.

"My whole life rushing past me in an instant."

"Please."

"Okay, okay, okay: I see a very old lady in funny clothes blowing poisoned darts at an elephant."

Kane replaced the card with another. "And this one?"

"Kafka talking to a bedbug."

"Correct."

"You're full of shit, do you know that?"

"*I* thought it was Kafka," Fell interjected, studying the card with interest.

"You wouldn't know Kafka from Bette Davis," Cutshaw accused him. "And you, you're a mental case," he told Kane.

"Yes, maybe I am."

Cutshaw rose and said, "Ingratiating bastard. Do you always play kiss-ass with the loonies?"

"No."

"I like you, Kane. You're regular."

Cutshaw tore the medal and chain from his neck and tossed them on the desk. "Here, take the medal. I'll take a book." He snatched *How I Believe* by Teilhard de Chardin.

"And now you'll be good for a week?" asked Kane.

"No. I'm an incorrigible liar." Cutshaw walked over to the door and threw it open with such force that again the crash loosened plaster from above. "May I go?" His voice had a childlike earnestness.

"Yes," said Kane.

"You're a very wise man, Van Helsing," said Cutshaw in an imitation of Dracula, "for one who has lived only one life." Then he loped out the door and disappeared from view.

Kane picked up the medal. "Saint Christopher," he murmured.

"Protect us," added Fell.

Kane turned the medal over, and he said without inflection, "There's something engraved on the back of it."

"Ora pro nobis?"

"'I am a Buddhist. In case of accident, call a lama.'"

Fell did not react. He picked up a book from the floor.

"What's Cutshaw's religion?" Kane asked.

"I don't know. Read the file; it's all in the file." Fell glanced at the title of the book he'd picked up. *Elementary Psychology*. He riffled its pages, noting marginal glosses and some heavy underlinings.

Kane took the book from Fell's hands and carried it to a bookshelf. From somewhere in the mansion, the voice of an inmate shrieked, "Fucking Venusians! *Clean up your act!*"

"You're a lucky man, Kane," sighed Fell.

"I am?"

"Well, it's one in a million, wouldn't you say: a man in the service who's properly assigned?"

"Aren't you?"

"I'm a pediatrician."

"I see," said Kane, stacking books.

"Oh, well, let's not carry on about it, Colonel. Take it easy!" Fell stooped to pick up some papers.

"We're all miscast," murmured Kane.

"What did you say? I didn't get that," said Fell, looking up.

Kane paused in his stacking, his face in shadow.

"Before Pearl Harbor, I thought I was going to be a priest. We're all miscast, one way or another. Just being born into this place . . ." His voice trailed off.

Fell waited, alert and intensely observant; his antic disposition had vanished. A keen intelligence shone from his eyes, a sense of caring. "Yes?" he prodded.

"I don't know," said Kane. His face was still hidden. "I think about sickness; earthquakes; wars." He lowered his head. "Painful death. The death of children. Children with cancer. If these are just part of our natural environment, why do they horrify us so? Why do we think of them as evil unless . . . we were programmed"—he felt for the words—"for someplace . . . else." His voice seemed far away. "Maybe conscience is our memory of how things were. Just suppose that we *haven't* evolved; that we've really been going backwards . . . more and more alienated from—" Here Kane stopped.

"From what?"

"Psychiatrists aren't supposed to say 'God.' "

"Betchyourass; it's going down on your record. Keep going."

"Maybe everything evil is a frustration, a separation from what we were meant for," Kane continued. "And maybe guilt is just the pain of that separation, that—that loneliness for God. We're fish out of water, Fell; maybe that's why men go mad."

For a time there was silence. When Kane spoke again, his voice was a whisper. "I don't think evil grows out of madness: I think madness grows out of evil."

A pair of gabardine pants flew into the room and hit Fell in the chest. "Well, here are my pants," he said matter-of-factly.

Cutshaw stood framed in the doorway. "Fromme has decided to give all his goods to the poor of brain." He glowered at Fell and then disappeared.

A shaggy and disreputable-looking mongrel dog trotted briskly into the room. It went to the desk and sniffed.

"What's this?" asked Kane.

The dog lifted a leg and piddled. "I think it's a dog," Fell said.

The dog seized the cuff of Fell's trousers in its jaws. It growled and tugged and Fell tugged back. "Goddammit, *not the pants!*" he yelled.

Suddenly the dog released its grip. It bolted to Kane and cowered behind him as an elfish inmate swooped into the room. He wore a tattered black cape atop his soiled green fatigues. He headed for the dog. "So *there* you are, you loafer!"

Groper raced into the room and pulled the inmate back. "I'm sorry, Colonel Kane," he said. "It's hard to keep track of these—"

"Please let him go," Kane told him.

"Sir?"

"Let go of him," Kane repeated. His voice was mild, but Groper felt inexplicably menaced. He relaxed his grip.

Kane added, "They may see me whenever they need to."

"You heard?" said Reno with satisfaction, fixing Groper with a glittering eye.

"Whatever you say, Colonel Kane," mumbled Groper. He turned and left quickly, glad to get away.

"That man is a lunatic and dangerous," Reno grumbled.

"Lieutenant David Reno, Colonel Hudson Kane," said Fell, introducing them. He put an arm around Reno's shoulder. "Reno is a navigator. B-52s." He squeezed Reno's shoulder with a comradely cheer and said, "That right, old buddy?"

"Fuck you." Reno glared at Fell with distaste.

"Is this your dog?" asked Kane, looking down.

"Does he look like my zebra? Christ, what the hell's *wrong* with you people?" The dog was licking Kane's shoe. Reno pointed. "Look, I think he likes you."

"What do you call him?"

"Irresponsible. He's ten minutes late for rehearsal. Now *out!*" Reno commanded the dog irritably. It padded from the room with a dignified mien, and in the background Kane caught a glimpse of Fairbanks nimbly sliding down a drape from the second floor.

Fell cleared his throat. "Lieutenant, the colonel might like to hear about your work."

Reno shriveled him with a glance. "Navigating? Child's play! I leave it to the crows, to the hawks, to the swallows! I am not a mere device! I am not an albino bat! Please watch your cup, dear heart, it's dripping."

"Not navigating," said Fell. "Your *work*. Tell the colonel."

"Ah! You speak of matters tender!"

"Lieutenant Reno," Fell explained, "is adapting Shakespeare's plays for dogs."

Reno drew up proudly. "A labor of love! A fucking headache! For God's sake, *somebody's* got to do it! Could you tell me your name again?"

"Hudson Kane."

"Too Jewish. We'll change it. Want to come to rehearsal?"

"What are you rehearsing?"

"We're doing that gripping scene in *Julius Caesar* where this noble-looking Dalmation wraps his toga around him—thusly!" Eyes aglow, he demonstrated with his cape. "And then he snarls: 'Et tu, White Fang?' "

Neither Kane nor Fell reacted. Slowly, Reno lowered the cape from before him, the mad grin of triumph melting from his face. Then he said, "You hate it."

"Not at all," Kane assured him quickly. "I think it's interesting."

"Good. We'll have to discuss it more fully later. In fact, I'd very much like your opinion on a problem I'm having with the casting of *Hamlet*. You see, if I put a Great Dane in the part, the fucking critics will accuse me of—"

Reno broke off as the dog barked urgently from outside the office door. " 'The time is out of joint,' " mourned Reno. "Shit, why do I have to live like this?

THE NINTH CONFIGURATION 29

One part and he's Barbra Streisand." He whipped the cape around him and rapidly moved for the door, calling, "Hold it! I'm coming, I'm *coming,* Rip Torn." At the door he turned and said to Kane, "Read the classics. It improves the whole respiratory system."

And then he was gone. They could hear him chiding the dog: "Where are your manners, Rip Torn? Where the hell were you raised, in a barn?"

Kane waited. Then he looked at Fell. "They're all that bad?"

"Or that ingenious."

"You believe that they're faking it, then."

"I don't know." Fell was sitting on the edge of Kane's desk. He tapped out a cigarette, lit it and swallowed smoke. "I've only been here about a week myself."

"That recently?"

"Sure." He took another drag. "The biggest mystery is Cutshaw, I guess."

"Why him?"

"Well, he wasn't in combat. So why should he fake it?"

Kane bowed his head and said softly, "Yes." He moved to a window and looked outside. A heavy fog shrouded the mansion.

"But then all these guys have high IQs," brooded Fell, "a few near genius, in fact; and most other fakery I've seen in the service comes under the category of falling out of parade in front of a reviewing stand and then urinating, preferably on some fieldgrade officer's leg."

Kane nodded.

"Their obsessions are just too ingenious," continued Fell. "They're too wild, too pat. But how is it that all these guys have obsessions? Are they in cahoots? Are Martians grabbing them? What the hell is it? And how do you say that a man like Bennish is pretending insanity to get out of combat? He holds the Congressional Medal of Honor. It just doesn't figure. I don't know. What do *you* think?"

Kane turned to reply, but instead merely stared

through the open door. Fell's eyes followed his gaze. Krebs was outside in the main hall, moving quickly, following Fairbanks, who was costumed as a nun, his fencing foil protruding from his robes, enormous round-lensed sunglasses on his face. He was carrying a large tin cup. Coins jangled inside it as he whirled on Krebs. "It is one of my multiple personalities," he growled. "I am Sister Eve Black." Krebs said something that neither Kane nor Fell could hear, but Fairbanks' reply was distinct: "The Little Sisters of the Poor is a recognized charity, Krebs. Fuck off!"

Fell closed the door and shook his head. "Fairbanks. There's another mysterioso." He sat down on a couch to the side, reaching over to an ashtray atop an end table. He stubbed out his cigarette. "Hell, who knows. He was flying that plane that we got from the British—you know, the one that takes off from the vertical and then flies straight? Twenty-four of them crashed for no damn reason; and right after number twenty-four is when Fairbanks started going to junior proms for trees. Hell, maybe we ought to give all of them electroshock treatment. That would shake out the fakers in a hurry, don't you think?" He saw Kane staring at the bottom of his boxer shorts, where the words "Vendome Liquors" were embroidered in red. "Or don't you?" Fell added.

Kane looked at him intently. "You remind me of someone."

"Who?"

"I don't know. You just seem so familiar to me. I suppose it will come to me."

"So will Ann Rutherford: just change your name to Andy Hardy." For a moment Kane continued to study him; then he stooped to pick up books and dossiers from the floor.

"Did you like my idea about electroshock treatment?" Fell asked.

"I thought you were joking."

"Me joke? You're not serious."

"I'll have to think about it."

"Yeah, think," said Fell. "Think hard. That's what you're paid for. Meantime, let me know when you come up with an answer." Kane nodded absently. Fell watched him for a moment, then opened the door and left. He went to his bedroom. Using a private line, he dialed a number that rang on a general's desk in the Pentagon. When it answered, Fell said, "He's here, sir."

Most of the fog had thinned away, but the evening was quickening. Rain clouds threatened. Kane sat at his desk, his eyes deep wells in a haggard face, a man with an urgent task, pursued. He had read the case histories of all the inmates and now was absorbed in a psychiatric textbook. He underlined frequently with a yellow soft-lead pencil. It was the evening of his arrival.

He adjusted the desk lamp, craning the light down closer to the book; then he lowered his head and rested his eyes, breathing deeply and noisily, almost asleep. He roused himself abruptly, rubbed his eyes and continued to read. He underlined a portion of the text. It dealt with the curative aspects of shock treatment. He studied it for a time. Then he glanced at Cutshaw's medal. It was still on his desk.

The office door flew open. It was Cutshaw, attired in swimming trunks, a beach towel over his shoulder. He wore a black armband and gripped the handle of a child's pail and shovel. His feet were shod in frogman's flippers and the swimming trunks and towel were patterned in a matching Polynesian motif. He slammed the office door behind him. "Let's go to the beach," he demanded.

Kane pushed the lamp head even lower, so that his face was hidden in darkness. "It's night and it's starting to rain," he said gently.

Cutshaw walked forward, the rubber flippers thwacking squeakily against the polished oaken floor. His brows were beetled together in a scowl. "I see you're *determined* to start an argument! Okay, then, let's play doctor."

"No."

"Then jacks; do you want to play jacks?"

"No, I don't."

"Good *Christ,* you don't want to do *anything!*" Cutshaw shrieked. "There's nothing to *do* around this place! I'm going *crazy!*"

"Cutshaw—"

"What do I have to do just to get in a word with you? Offer sacrifice? Well, here then!" He upended the beach pail onto Kane's desk and then lifted it off and tossed it away, disclosing a mound of shaped damp earth atop an open dossier. "I've brought you a mud pie; *now* can I talk to you?"

"Will you talk about the moon?"

"Listen, everyone *knows* the moon is Roquefort; I've come here to talk about Colonel Fell."

"What about him?"

"What *about* him? Are you a *stone?* Christ. Captain Nammack approached him this morning complaining of a strange and wondrous malady, and do you know what that quack prescribed? He said, 'Here, take this. It's a suicide pill with a mild laxative side effect.' What kind of bedside manner is that?"

"What's wrong with Nammack?" Kane asked softly.

"He's got a tipped uterus."

"I see."

"Tell that to Nammack and see if it comforts him in his agony. What shall I tell him? 'Listen, Nammack, take it easy? I've talked to Colonel Kane and while he sympathizes with you, he says to stuff your fucking uterus with suicide pills and aspirin, seeing as Fell is erratic but fair'? And that he also said, 'I see'?" The astronaut switched to a whining tone. "Let's go to the beach," he repeated. "Come *on!*" He attempted to stamp his foot in pout and the rubber flipper cracked like a whip against the floor.

"It's dark and it's raining," Kane replied.

Cutshaw's face contorted into rage. He picked up the beachpail shovel from the desk and broke it in two with a splintery snap. "There I *break* the arrow of peace!" He flung away the pieces. "Son of a bitch! Listen, who the hell are you? I'm starting to think that you're Fairbanks in some fucking new weirdo disguise. He came around once in the skin of a caribou, but we recognized him, the jerk. Do you know what we did to him then? We gave him the silent treatment! Hell, we didn't even nod to him, that insolent, antlered schmuck. Finally he split." The astronaut's eyes narrowed as he scrutinized Kane. "Are you really a Catholic?" he asked.

"Yes."

"Tough shit. I'm a Flaming Knight Rampant of the Christian Hussars. Would you like to ask me what we believe in?"

"What do you believe in?"

"That colonels consort with elks. Now get out of here, Hud! I'm losing patience with you swiftly!"

"You want me to leave?" Kane asked him.

Cutshaw lunged over the desk and seized Kane's wrist. "Are you mad?" His eyes bulged wide in fear. "And lose the only friend I've *got?*" he cried. "Oh, God, don't do it, Hud, please! Don't go away! Don't leave me alone in this house of horrors!"

The colonel's eyes welled up with pity. "No, I won't go away, I promise. Sit down. Sit down and we'll talk," he said soothingly.

"Yes!" shrieked Cutshaw. "I want to talk! I want therapy!" He released Kane's wrist and was instantly calm again. He flapped his way to the couch against the wall, where he flung himself down and stretched out on his back, staring up at the ceiling. "God, where do I begin?"

"Free-associate," Kane suggested.

Cutshaw turned and eyed him severely. He got up off the couch, thumped over to the desk and recovered his medal, then returned to the couch and lay supine. "And now a few words about my childhood. I was born in North Dakota in a tiny—"

"Your records say Brooklyn," said Kane.

"Listen, I'll come over there—okay?—and you come lie down here and we'll see how well *you* do! Whose therapy is this?"

"Yours," said Kane.

"Can't I ask a rhetorical question without some ass-hole trying to *answer* it? Be *quiet!*" Cutshaw shouted. He flipped over on his belly. "I had three maiden aunts," he recited calmly. "Their names were Ugly, Vulgar and Tawdry, and every Christmas they'd buy me a Monopoly game from a thrift shop, except that the board was always missing: I never had a fucking board. Sure, I finally made one, but how does it sound: 'Go directly to jackknife and do not pass frog'? Hell, I never even *saw* a proper board until I was almost twenty, and I had to put *ice* on the back of my neck to stop trembling! Ah, well, screw it; so I never had a board. But I'd never use that as a cop-out, Hud, that Jack the Ripper bullshit. Yeah, sure: Jack the Ripper was misunderstood. At the age of six he had a lucky knife called 'Rosebud' and somebody stole it, so Jack spent the rest of his lifetime looking for it, but Jack had this silly idea that the knife had been hidden in some-one's *throat*. Now, do you *buy* that crap? You can an-swer."

"No," said Kane.

"You're funny that way. There were kids on my block who tortured caterpillars; they'd cut them up and burn them. And you know why they did it? Because they were bastards. Every mean insensitive grown-up bastard *started* as a bastard. Show me a kid who tortures caterpillars and I'll show you a son of a bitch. Do you approve? I crave approval. I *need* approval. I would rather have approval than a jelly roll with yogurt. Incidentally, have you noticed that Groper never showers? It's because we'd see the caterpillar blood on his legs? The hateful bastard! He's a regular Santa Claus: every Christmas he jumps in his sled and delivers napalm to the poor. That son of a bitch. A dumb stray dog with a coiled-up tail came up and whined and licked his shoe one day on the drawbridge, and Groper right away whipped out a jackknife and sliced the dog's tail off, cropped it real close, and the dog is screaming and going crazy and then Groper says he helped it on account of the fleas; they collect in the tail. Christ, he's up to his *knees* in caterpillar blood! You know, he used to be a writer for *Time* magazine and for years he always talked in captions: he was always saying, 'After the melon, a grape,' and things like that in the fucking mess hall. Also, he loved to say 'brouhaha.' But that was in the old days, Hud. I mean, now he only does it when he drinks. The poor slob was a colonel once, did you know that? Then he said 'brouhaha' in front of MacArthur and they busted him back to major. Wake up. Are you awake?" The astronaut turned for a look at Kane.

"Yes, I'm awake," said Kane.

"So I see; but you were nodding, Catherine Earnshaw." Cutshaw flopped over on his back once again and then queried, "What do you think of asps?"

"Asps?"

"You are absolutely incapable of giving a man a straight answer!" Cutshaw produced a lollipop from a pocket and began to lick at it noisily.

"Cutshaw, why do you wear that armband?"

"Because I'm in mourning."

"For whom?"

"For God." Cutshaw sat up, removed the flippers and threw them down. "That's right." Now he threw away the lollipop. "I don't belong to the God Is Alive and Living in Argentina Club." Cutshaw stood up and began to pace in agitation. *"Basta!* No more talk about God! Wrap it up, that's enough. Let's get back to psychiatry." He paused by the desk. "That reminds me. Some psychiatrist! You haven't even asked me if I have obsessions."

"Do you?"

"Yes, I do. I hate feet. Christ, I can't stand the *sight* of them. How could a so-called beautiful God give us ugly padding things like feet!"

"So you can walk."

"I don't want to walk, I want to fly! Feet are disfiguring and disgraceful." Cutshaw looked down at his own bare feet, strode over to the couch, sat down and tugged the flippers back on. "If God exists," he said, "he's a fink. Or more likely a foot: a giant, omniscient, omnipotent Foot. Do you think that is blasphemous?"

"Yes, I do."

"I believe that I capitalized the *F.*"

The astronaut studied Kane as though attempting to evaluate him. "How many times," he asked him finally, "can a person break a shish kebab skewer in half?" He stood up on the couch, reached out for the mounted head of a boar, and gripping its tusks, began to sway gently back and forth in midair. "Everything has parts," he continued, in that posture. "The skewer has parts. Now, how many times can I break it in half? An infinite number of times or only a limited number of times? If the answer's an infinite number of times, then the skewer must be infinite. Which is moose piss, why don't we face it. But if I can only cut the skewer in half for a *limited* number of times . . . if I get down to a piece of skewer that can no longer be cut in half —I mean, assuming I were Foot and could do anything I wanted—then I'm down to a piece of skewer that has no parts. But if it has no parts, it can't exist! Am I right? No. I see it in your eyes. You think I'm a crazy old man."

"Not at all," responded Kane. "You have merely failed to distinguish between the real and mental orders. Mentally—or theoretically—there isn't any limit at all on how many times you can halve that skewer; but in the *real* order of things—or in other words, practically speaking—you would finally come to a point where, when you cut the skewer in half, the halves would convert themselves into energy."

"Foot, you are wise!" breathed the astronaut. Something gleamed in his eyes. He dropped to the floor with a rubbery thwack, went over to the desk and replaced the medal in front of Kane. "You pass," he said. "Now can you prove that there is a Foot?"

"I simply believe it," said Kane.

"Can you *prove* it?"

"There are some arguments for reason."

"Oh, are those the same things that we used to justify dropping atomic bombs on Japan? If they are, *fuck them!*" Cutshaw leaned over and spread the contents of the bucket all over Kane's desk. "Here, draw diagrams in the dirt." He threw himself face down on the couch. "This had better be good," he warned, a cushion muffling his voice.

"There is a biochemical argument," Kane said tentatively. "It isn't a proof, exactly. . . ."

Cutshaw turned on his side, yawned elaborately and checked his watch.

"In order for life to have appeared spontaneously on earth," Kane resumed, "there first had to be in existence a protein molecule of a certain dyssymmetrical configuration, the configuration point nine. But according to the laws of probability, for one of these molecules to appear by chance alone would require a volume of matter of more than—well—many trillions and trillions of times that of the size of the entire known universe; and considered strictly from the angle of time—"

"Timewise."

"Considered from the angle of time, and given a volume of matter equivalent to the earth's, such a probability would require ten to the two hundred and something power billions of years—a number with so many zeros in it you couldn't fit them into a book the size of *The Brothers Karamazov*. And that's just *one* molecule. For life to appear, you would have to have *millions* in existence and *at roughly the same time*. Which I find more fantastic than simply believing in a God."

Cutshaw sat up. "Are you finished?"

"Yes."

Cutshaw stood up and went to the door, where he turned and said cryptically, "Tawdry Groper eats unblessed venison." Then he turned again and strode from view.

The crash of a hammer pounding plaster resounded through the wall. Kane walked out of his office. To the right of the door he saw Fairbanks, wearing an Air Force high-altitude helmet. He was holding a short-handled sledgehammer and was glaring at a hole in the wall. Groper raced up to him, cursing. "I *hid* it, goddammit, I *hid* it!" He ripped the hammer from Fairbanks' hand. "How the hell did you find it?" he yelled.

"I wouldn't *dare* tell you *that*," said Fairbanks. He whipped the hammer back out of Groper's clutch and told him, "Kindly stand aside."

"You little—"

Groper had lifted an arm as though to strike him, when Kane intervened. "Major Groper!"

"Sir, he's been—"

"I don't care *what* he's done; you are not to lay hands on any of these men at any time for any reason."

"But, Colonel—"

Groper was about to say more, but as his eyes looked into Kane's, he broke off, took a step backward, saluted stiffly and retreated to his quarters.

Kane regarded the inmate kindly. "You're Captain Fairbanks," he said.

"Not today."

"I'm sorry. I was sure you were—"

"Not today. Understand me? Multiple personality. 'My house has many mansions.' "

"Yes."

"I am Dr. Franz von Pauli."

Kane put a fatherly arm around his shoulder. Far

down the hall he caught a glimpse of Cutshaw staring at them from the dormitory door. Kane looked at the hole gouged out of the wall and said, "Why did you do that, Captain Fairbanks?"

"I beg your pardon?"

"Why did you do that to the wall?"

"I thought you were kidding." The inmate's eyes were intense and pale blue and set in an innocent pudgy face that belonged at a junior college tea dance. "I do it," he replied, "in the interest of science and nucleonics; because I'm *convinced* we can walk through walls! Not just me; I mean anyone. Cops. People. People in Nashville. It's the *spaces!* The empty spaces between the atoms in my body—or yours: you don't mind my getting personal? No. If it gets you uptight, let me know."

"Go ahead."

"You got a headache?"

Kane had winced as though in reaction to a sudden, stabbing pain, lowering his head and pinching the bridge of his nose. His eyes were closed. "No," he said softly.

"Terrific. Look, it's all in the size of the empty spaces between the atoms in that wall: when you look at it relative to the size of the atoms themselves—well, the size of the spaces is immense! It's like the distance, frankly speaking, between the earth and the planet Mars, and—"

"Come to the point, please, Captain Fairbanks," said Kane in a voice that reflected strain, yet was not unkind.

"What's the hurry?" asked Fairbanks. "The atoms won't leave. Hell, they're not going *any*place."

"Yes."

"Colonel, atoms can be *smashed;* they cannot *fly!*"

Kane reacted to something like pain again.

"Do you have to go toy-toy?" asked Fairbanks. "Number two?"

Kane shook his head.

"Listen, don't be ashamed; we're only human."

Kane lowered his arm from the inmate's shoulder. "Tell me why you strike the wall."

"You're dogged. I like that: dogged but fair. Now listen. The spaces—the same immense and empty spaces between the atoms in that wall exist between the atoms in your body as well! So walking *through* the wall is merely a matter of gearing the holes between the atoms in my body to the holes between the atoms in that wall! That naughty stubborn fucking—"

Fairbanks ended his statement with another great swing of his hammer. Plaster flew out in all directions. He looked sullen; he stared at the hole he had just produced. "Nothing," he muttered. Then he looked at Kane. "I keep experimenting, see. I concentrate hard. I try to exert the full force of my mind on the atoms in my body so they'll mix and rearrange; so they'll fit just *exactly* those spaces in the wall. And then I try the experimental method—I try to walk through the wall. Like now. I just took a running dash, and I failed —*horribly!*"

He swung once more at the wall and another hole gaped forth. "Stuck-up cunts," he muttered.

"Why did you do that?" asked Kane.

"I am punishing the atoms! I am making of them an example! An object lesson! A thing! So when the others see what's coming—when they see I'm not kidding around—why, they'll fall into line! They'll let me pass through!" Fairbanks accompanied the end of his statement with another vicious swing. "Independent snots!" he said, glaring at the wall. "Shape up or ship out!"

"May I?" asked Kane, gently lifting the hammer from the inmate's grasp.

"Sure!" growled Fairbanks. "Swing! Enjoy! Maybe they'll *listen* to a stranger!"

"I had something else in mind."

The inmate looked outraged and grabbed for the hammer. First he gave a tug and then a vigorous pull; but the hammer did not move from Kane's grip. He looked down at the hammer, and then up at Kane, his eyes a little fuddled. "Your grip is very strong," he said at last.

"I think," said Kane, "that your problem may lie in the properties of the hammer: some nuclear imbalance impinging on the ions."

"Interesting theory," said Fairbanks.

"Would you mind if I kept the hammer for study?"

Suddenly Fairbanks began to scream. He struggled furiously to regain the hammer. Krebs and Christian appeared and restrained him. He was hysterical.

"Medication is indicated here," said Kane.

"I'll have to find Colonel Fell," Krebs told him. "I haven't seen him."

"Who else has a key to the drug locker?"

"No one," said Krebs. Fairbanks kept shrieking. His eyes bulged out.

"Not even a medical orderly?" asked Kane.

"No, sir. Not since we had the pilferage, sir."

"From the drug locker? What was taken?"

"The colonel's Cadbury Fruit and Nut bars, sir. He stores them there." He paused and then added, "It's the temperature, sir."

Kane released the hammer and Fairbanks subsided. "There may be a recurrence," Kane said softly. "You'd better find him."

"Yes, sir."

Fairbanks looked puzzled. "Where the fuck did this hammer come from?" he asked. Kane slipped it from his grasp and Krebs and Christian led the inmate away. Kane stood rooted, looking down at the hammer in his hands. Then he clutched at his head.

Groper was watching him from the second floor, where he stood by the balustrade. Kane looked up at him as if he had known he was being watched. Groper walked quickly toward his bedroom.

Back in his office, Kane again immersed himself in study. Outside it was raining and somewhere a clock tolled nine. Kane looked up and stared at the window as the rain battered against it in sheets. Someone came into the room. It was Krebs.

"Captain Fairbanks is still okay, sir."

"Good. Where's Colonel Fell? Have you found him?"

Krebs hesitated, then said, "No, sir. But he hasn't checked out, so he must be on the grounds."

Kane's face was tense and pained for a moment; then he said, "When you find him, please tell him to come to me right away. I need to see him."

"Yes, sir." Krebs did not leave. He stood looking at Kane.

"That's all, Krebs. Thank you," said Kane at last.

"About Colonel Fell, sir," said Krebs.

"Yes?"

Krebs was hesitant. "I think he covers up, sir."

"What do you mean?"

"Well, I think things hurt him a lot, sir. You know—sick people; patients dying on him. I wouldn't want you to think badly of him, sir. I think he does what he does to take his mind off things."

Kane stared at him for a while; then he felt at his brow and said, "I see."

"Have you got a headache, sir? I can get you some aspirin, sir, if that will help."

"That's very kind of you, Krebs. I'm all right. Good night."

"Good night, sir," said Krebs.

"Please close the door behind you."

"Yes, sir."

Kane returned to his reading and note-taking. Hours passed. Fell did not appear. The rain was torrential, slamming at the windows. Kane squinted at the words he was reading, blinking, straining to see. Finally, he could not keep his eyes open any longer and he laid down his head on his folded arms. He slept.

And dreamed. Rain. A jungle. He was hunted. He had killed someone. Who? He was kneeling by the body. He turned it over, but the head stayed facing down and blood gushed out of a headless neck. Then a man with a Z-shaped scar on his brow said, "For Christ's sake, Colonel, let's get the hell out of here!" He plucked a white mouse from out of the air and the mouse became a pure white lily stained with blood. Then Kane was on the surface of the moon. There was a lunar landing craft to the right, and an astronaut, Cutshaw, moving, drifting, through the atomosphere, until at last he extended his arms beseechingly up to a crucified Christ at the left. The figure of Christ had the face of Kane. Then the dream became lucid. He dreamed he awakened in his office and Billy Cutshaw was sitting on his desk, eying him intently while lighting a cigarette. Kane said, "What is it? What do you want?"

"It's about my brother, Lieutenant Reno. You've got to help him."

"Help? How?"

"Reno is possessed of a devil, Hud. He is levitating nightly and he also talks to dogs, which is not entirely natural. I want you to cast out his demons. You're a colonel and a Catholic and an unfrocked priest."

Suddenly Reno was in the room, floating three feet off the floor. He was wearing a high-altitude flight suit. He looked at Kane and opened his mouth and out came the yappings of a dog.

Kane put a finger to his neck and felt a round Roman collar. He experienced a surging exhilaration.

It was then that the dream again changed in texture, and seemed to be not a dream at all. Cutshaw was staring at him intently, his cigarette glowing in the dimness. "You awake?" said the apparition.

Kane moved his lips and tried to say "Yes," but no sound would issue forth. He spoke with his mind, thinking—saying?—"Yes."

"Do you really believe in an afterlife?"

"Yes."

"I mean, *really*."

"Yes, I believe."

"Why?"

"I just know."

"Blind faith?"

"No, not that; not that, exactly."

"How do you *know?*" insisted Cutshaw.

Kane paused, dredging for arguments. Then at last he said (thought?): "Because every man who has ever lived has been filled with desire for perfect happiness. But unless there is an afterlife, fulfillment of this desire is impossible. Perfect happiness, in order to be perfect, must carry with it the assurance that the happiness won't cease; that it will not be snatched away. But no one has ever had such assurance; the mere fact of death serves to contradict it. Yet why should Nature implant in everyone a desire for something unattainable? I can think of no more than two answers: either Nature is consistently mad and perverse; or after this life there's another, a life where this universal desire for perfect happiness can be fulfilled. But nowhere else in creation does Nature exhibit this kind of perversity; not when it comes to a basic drive. An eye is always for seeing and an ear is always for hearing. And any universal craving—I mean a craving without exceptions —has to be capable of fulfillment. It can't be fulfilled *here,* so it's fulfilled, I think, somewhere else; some*time* else. Does that make any sense? It's difficult. I think I'm dreaming. Am I dreaming?"

Cutshaw's cigarette briefly glowed bright. "If you dream, don't drive," he rasped. And then Kane was on the island of Molokai, where he had come to cure the lepers, but it somehow was also an orphanage where a Franciscan monk was lecturing to children in military uniform, their faces blank and eroded. Suddenly the roof fell in upon them as bombs struck Molokai. "Get out! There's still time! Get out!" cried the monk. "No, I'm staying with you!" cried out the Kane in the dream. The Franciscan's head came loose from his body and Kane picked it up and kissed it fervently. Then he hurled it away in revulsion. The head said, "Feed my sheep."

Kane awakened with an inchoate shout. He wasn't in his office. He was fully dressed and sitting on the floor in a corner of his bedroom. He could not remember how he had gotten there.

Reno awakened at dawn and looked at Cutshaw's cot. It was empty. He slipped on fatigues and walked down the aisle past the cots and footlockers and out of the dormitory. All the other inmates were sleeping.

Reno searched the mansion, looking for Cutshaw, then went outside and padded through the fog. He stopped and looked around the desolate courtyard once and bitterly muttered, "Fardels!" At last he saw him. The astronaut was lurking in the lower branches of a spruce where Groper customarily stood before Assembly. He was stirring a gallon of paint balanced between his knees. Reno scuttled up the tree trunk and parted a branch. "Captain Billy!" he exclaimed.

"For Christ's sake, keep your voice down!" Cutshaw said guardedly. "What in the hell are you doing up here?"

"It's Kane!" whispered Reno excitedly. His eyes were shining and wild. He was hyperventilating.

"What about him?" Cutshaw retorted, picking a pine needle out of the paint.

"Billy, none of him is him!"

"Meaning what?"

"Kane is Gregory Peck in *Spellbound,* Billy! He comes to take charge of a nuthouse and it turns out the guy's really crazy himself!"

Cutshaw exhaled a weary sigh. Even among the mansion inmates it was generally conceded that Reno entertained a number of obsessions more magnificent than most. Once he had reported that while strolling "jaunty-jolly" through the grounds on a moonless night, he had detected "hissing from above," and looking up, spied Major Groper "crouched amidst the fronds of a palm tree," deep in whispered conversation with a giant black-and-white owl. Nothing had shaken him from this story. When Cutshaw had reminded him that the estate was visibly barren of any variety of palm tree, Reno had eyed him pityingly and said in soft rebuttal, "Anyone with money can pull out a tree. And then certain parties could very easily fill in the hole."

From that day forward, Reno was ignored. There was only one way to be rid of him, and that was to walk away.

Cutshaw looked down. It was a twenty-foot drop.

"Kane is Gregory Peck," Reno said again. "Last night in the middle of the night, I wake up and there's cookies in my teeth, raisins and crap; so I go to the clinic, see, for some dental floss, and who do I see on his arse like he's in some kind of trance or something?" Reno began to imitate the scene, his hands moving in dazed but purposeful action: picking something up; throwing something down; picking something up; throwing something—

Cutshaw interrupted the performance. He pointed to the ground: "Down! Get down! I want you to fall like an overripe mango!"

"There's also another possibility, Billy. The drug-chest door was sitting wide open. He could have been bombed on something."

"Scram!"

"Lots of doctors get hooked on drugs," Reno argued

reasonably. "Lots of psychiatrists are deeply disturbed. You know that. They've got the highest suicide rate of any profession there is, and that's a fact, you can check that, Billy."

Cutshaw paused at this, an eyebrow lifting cautiously. "When did this happen?" he asked.

"About three in the morning. I swear it. Listen, here's the capper, the proof, here's what he does! It was just like Gregory Peck in *Spellbound,* Billy. It was just like the movie, exactly! I go and get a fork. Understand? I get a fork and also a tablecloth from the mess! I put down the tablecloth in front of him, with the fork I made some ski tracks on it, and he *fainted!* Just like *Gregory Peck in the movie!*"

Cutshaw pointed to the ground again, gritting, "Get down! You hear me? Get—" He broke off suddenly and put a finger to his lips and a hand over Reno's mouth. Then he looked below and tilted the gallon can of paint so that its contents spilled out smoothly.

From below, the voice of Groper rumbled upward: "You son of a bitch!"

"Can I talk now?" Reno asked.

"Yes, go ahead." Cutshaw beamed, satisfied.

"I forgot to mention one thing: Kane had a cat with three heads on his lap. He might have been stroking it."

"Get down!"

"You're right, it was on top of his head."

"Get *down!*"

Reno looked at Groper. "I think I'll go up."

Fell appeared for breakfast in the mess reserved for the staff, a room off the kitchen, with a fireplace. He sat down opposite Kane. There was no one else there yet.

Fell was cheery and refreshed and he held out his coffee cup to Kane, who had the pot in his hand.

"I heard you were looking for me," said Fell.

"That's right; where were you?"

"Just walking around."

"In the rain?"

"Was it raining?"

"Captain Fairbanks was in need of sedation last night. Please make up a duplicate key to the drug chest. I had to break into it."

March 23. Kane was sitting at his desk when Groper burst in upon him, a letter in his hand.

"Look at this, sir." Groper handed Kane the letter, retaining the envelope. "Colonel, read that. Would you read that?"

Kane looked down at the typewritten letter. He read:

To my darling, my dearest, my flaming secret love: How I've hungered for this moment when I might tear away the mask and unburden by aching, bleeding heart. My sweetest, I saw you but an instant, a *semi*-instant; yet I knew I was your slave. Wondrous creature, I adore you! You are sandalwood from Nineveh, you are truffles from the Moon! In my dreams I am a madman! Yes! I rip away your dress, and then your bra, and then your glasses, and I—

Kane looked up from the letter. "What is the point of this, Major Groper?"

"Look at the signature, sir," said Groper, quelling his

uneasiness in Kane's presence. The signature was "Major Marvin Groper." Beneath it was a postscript that stated: "You know where to find me, baby." There followed the telephone number of the center.

"Sir, I got phone call after phone call this morning from broads who got letters like this one," Groper ranted.

Kane held up the letter. "Where did you get this?" he asked.

"Well, some of them—"

"Some of whom?"

"Well, I mean, these women, sir."

"Which women?"

"Well, they happened to come by here today and they—"

" 'Happened'?"

"Well, no, sir; I asked them—the ones with nice voices—and—"

"Groper?"

"They're *ugly*, sir! Ugly as *sin!*" erupted Groper in a sudden release of frustration and anger. "And I think that the bastard who wrote all those letters needs some kind of punishment and restriction!"

"Who wrote them?"

"Look at the envelope, Colonel." Groper set it down in front of him. "There's only one mind here that would have done this!"

The address on the envelope looked carbonish and blurred and it gave the impression of being part of a mass commercial mailing. The addressee was designated simply as "Occupant."

"Sir, you've got to *talk* to him!" Groper was extremely distraught.

Kane said, "All right. I'll see him. Bring him to me."

Both sides of the inmates' dormitory were neatly lined with wash basins, cots and footlockers. In the aisle between them, Cutshaw paced back and forth nervously while some of the men wrote more letters. Fairbanks approached him, holding one in his hand. "This is a classic," he said. "Does the best one get a prize?"

"Leslie, *heaven* will reward you," Cutshaw said moodily.

"I think we should have some kind of incentive."

"Leslie Morris, I just gave you one."

"Your incentive reeks of socialism. Freaking *creeping* socialism." Fairbanks' hand flew swiftly to his sword.

"You'd draw your sword on Captain Billy?"

"I am merely holding the hilt."

A breathless Reno had burst into the dormitory and now irrupted between them. "Captain Billy, I saw it again!"

"Saw *what* again?"

"The owl that talks to Groper. It wears a party hat; you can't miss it."

"Go to *Titus Andronicus,*" Cutshaw growled. "Star in it. Bake yourself in a pie."

"That's blasphemy!"

Reno saw Groper bearing down on Cutshaw from behind, and pointing imperiously at Cutshaw, he demanded of Groper: "Guard! *Seize* him!"

"The Man in the Iron Mask," snapped Cutshaw. When he turned and saw Groper, he beamed with pleasure. "Damn well about time," he said.

Groper led Cutshaw to the office and Kane confronted him with the letter addressed to "Occupant." "Did you write it?" he asked.

"Are we going to have a scene, Hud?" Cutshaw spread-eagled his arms in a sacrificial gesture, a forearm striking Groper's face. "Yes! *I wrote the letter!* Now shoot me for giving the spinster hope! Love to the loveless! Depravity to the deprived! Never mind the space race, Hud! Feed me to the giant ants! Go ahead! Make widows of five hundred pen pals!"

"Purely a pleasure," breathed Groper.

Cutshaw leaned in closer to Kane, and lowered his voice to a whisper. "Sir, I've noticed an exotic odor in here, and being as you're a colonel, sir, it's got to be Major—"

Groper moved in to him menacingly and Cutshaw leaped behind Kane, shouting, "Don't let him touch me! I'm crazy!"

"Sure you're crazy!" Groper moved on Cutshaw again.

"Groper!" Kane said firmly.

Groper halted. "Yes, sir!"

Cutshaw bent over in the posture of a hunchback and croaked in a coarsened, Slavic voice, "Hah! Dey try to kill Igor! But Igor still live and now *dey* dead!" The astronaut swayed a bit.

Groper advanced again.

"Major Groper!"

"Yes, sir!" Groper stopped. He was quivering visibly. His eyes were scarlet streaks.

"Have you been drinking?" Kane asked quietly.

Groper shouted, *"Yes!"* He was hysterical.

"Try to control yourself, Major."

"But my God, you should have *seen* those broads! Ugly! *Ugly!* Jesus *Christ!"*

Kane stood up. "Major Groper—"

The room trembled with the vibration of a hammer blow and Groper turned pale. "Where did he get it?" he yipped. He turned fiery eyes on Cutshaw. "You! *You* got it for him!" Groper saw the look in Kane's eyes, the force. He quivered with helplessness and frustration, then verged on tears. "He can keep it!" he quavered, backing out of the room. "You hear? He can *keep* the fucking thing! He can keep it!" Groper fled from the office.

Cutshaw stared after him, eyebrows furrowed. "Well, I'll be a son of a bitch," he said softly. He turned, hearing Kane on the phone with Fell.

"Do what you can with him," Kane was saying. He was sitting down. "A sedative, perhaps. But watch him." He paused, then said, "No—not an ice pack." He hung up the phone.

Cutshaw prowled over to the desk. "Are you Gregory Peck?" he demanded. "What's the story?"

Kane did not answer.

Cutshaw's eyes narrowed to slits. "Proud ox, we will teach you the error of false pride." He whipped a document out of his pocket and pressed it flat on the desk in front of Kane, and demanded: "Here, sign this confession, Hud! Or Greg! Or Tab! Or whoever you are!"

Kane looked at the paper and remarked, "This is blank."

"Of course it's blank," growled Cutshaw. "I'm still not certain who you are. Look, I'm doing this for Reno," he explained. "Just sign and we'll fill it in later. Go ahead," he advised. "Plead the mercy of the court. Kangaroos can be kind. Kangaroos are not all bad. Just sign it so we can show it to Reno and then maybe we can all get a little bit of peace."

"If I sign it, will you make a confession too?"

"I'm listening."

"Why won't you go to—"

Before he could finish the question, Cutshaw roared, "Silence when you're speaking to me!" Then he took a step back and looked portentous. "I know who you are," he warned.

"Who am I?"

"You're an unfrocked priest." Cutshaw flung himself onto the couch and sprawled on his back. He said, "I want you to hear my confession, Father No-Face."

Kane said softly, "I'm not a priest."

"Then who the hell are you?"

For a moment Kane stared like a man recollecting something unexpected. He touched his collar lightly.

"I'm Colonel Kane."

"You're Gregory Peck, you dumb ass; don't let anyone talk you out of it! See, if you're captured they'll try to do that brainwashing crap and make you think that you're Adolphe Menjou or maybe even Warren Beatty. Now me, I would *love* to be Warren Beatty!"

"I don't see why," said Kane.

"Of course you don't see why! You're Gregory Peck!"

"I see."

"Like hell. You patronizing snot." Abruptly, Cutshaw sat up on the couch. "You aren't Gregory Peck at all; you're an unfrocked priest," he accused with contempt. "Incidentally, old padre, I've got some rather disquieting news for you: I can prove that there's a Foot. . . . Would you like me to do it for you now or would you prefer to wire the Pope before I talk to Associated Press? Because once that happens, Hud, I warn you, there won't be frocks to go around. Better put yours on now so they'll think you're sincere."

"I would like to hear your proof."

"Put on the frock, Hud. I don't want to see you hurt."

"Let me hear the proof."

"You crazy, stubborn kid, Hud. Don't come sniveling to me later when you can't get a job cleaning altars." Cutshaw stood up and began to pantomime tennis serves. "Have you ever heard of 'entropy'? Say it's a race horse and I'll maim you."

"It is related," said Kane, "to a law of thermodynamics."

"Pretty slick there, Hud. Maybe too slick for your own damn good. Now where am I heading?" demanded Cutshaw.

"You tell me."

"To where the *universe* is heading. To a final, final heat death. Do you know what that is? Well, Hud, I'll tell you. I am Morris the Explainer. It's a basic foos of physics, an *irreversible* basic foos, that one of these days, by and by, the whole damn party will be over. In about three billion years every particle of matter in the entire universe will be totally disorganized. Random, totally random. And once the universe is random it'll maintain a certain temperature, a certain *constant* temperature, that never, never changes. And because it never changes, the particles of matter in the universe can never hope to reorganize. The universe can't build up again. Random; it'll always stay random. Forever and ever and ever. Doesn't that scare the living piss out of you, Hud? Hud, where's your frock? Got a spare? Let me have it. I shouldn't talk like this in front of me. I swear, it gives me the willies." Cutshaw stopped pantomiming serves and flopped on the couch, where he curled up in the fetal position.

"Please continue," Kane prodded.

"Do you accept my foos of physics?"

"Yes, I accept it."

Cutshaw scowled, looking up. "Don't say 'it,' okay? Say 'foos.' Say, 'I accept your basic foos.' "

"I accept your basic foos," said Kane.

"Good. Now follow." Cutshaw's speech became slow and measured. "It's a matter of *time* before it happens, before we reach that final heat death. And when we reach that final heat death, life can never reappear. If that seems clear, Hud, paw the ground twice."

"That's clear."

"Okay. Now, let's take a simple disjunction. Either matter—matter or energy—is eternal and always existed, or it *didn't* always exist and had a definite beginning in time. So let's eliminate one or the other. Let's say that matter always existed. And bear in mind that the coming heat death, Hud, is purely a matter of time. Did I say three billion years? Let's say a *billion* billion years. I don't care *what* the time required is, Hud. Whatever it is, it's limited. But if matter always existed, you and I aren't here—do you see? We simply don't *exist!* Heat death has already come and gone!"

"I don't follow."

"Of course. You'd rather confess. Give me the frock and I'll let you confess. Let no one write 'Obdurate' on my tombstone. Call me flexible, Hud, and confess."

"Captain—"

"Warren, then. Call me Warren."

"I've missed a connection," said Kane, "in the argument."

"My next impression: a human fly." Cutshaw shot up from the couch, flew at a wall and made a number of earnest attempts at running straight up its side. After his fifth abortive try, he stood and glowered at the wall. "Fairbanks is right," he muttered, vexed. "Something is wrong with these fucking walls." Then he glared at Kane. "You've been missing connections the whole of your life. Foot! You are dumber than a prize dauphin. Look: if matter has always existed and if heat death is a matter of time—like, let's say, a billion billion years —then, Hud, it's got to have already *happened!* A billion billion years have come and gone a trillion times, an *infinite* number of times! Ahead of us and behind us is an infinite number of years in the case of matter always existing. So heat death has already come and gone! And once it comes, there can never be life! Never again! Not for eternity! So how come we're talking, huh? How come? Though notice that I am talking *sensibly* while you just sit there *drooling*. Nevertheless, we are here. Why is that?"

Interest quickened in Kane's eyes. "Either matter is not eternal, I'd say, or the entropy theory is wrong."

"What? You reject my basic foos?"

"No, I don't."

"Then there can be only one alternative, Greg: matter *hasn't* always existed. Which means that at one time—or before time began—there was absolutely nothing—*nothing*—in existence. So how come there's something *now?* The answer is obvious to even the lowliest, the meanest, of intelligences, and that, of course, means you. The answer is that something *other* than matter had to make matter begin to be. That something other I call Foot. How does that grab you?"

"It's very compelling."

"There's only one thing wrong," said Cutshaw. "I don't believe it for a minute. What do you take me for, a lunatic?" The astronaut walked up to the desk. "You're so dumb, you're adorable," he said. "I copied that proof from a privy wall at a Maryknoll Mission in Beverly Hills."

"It doesn't convince you?"

"Intellectually, yes; but emotionally—no. And *that*," he concluded, "is the problem."

He marched to the door and turned. "Incidentally," he demanded, "what were you doing in the clinic in the middle of the night?" He stood there, waiting for some reaction; but there was none; no change of expression.

"What are you looking for, Cutshaw?" Kane asked him.

"Joe DiMaggio," Cutshaw said, and walked out slowly.

Kane stayed in the office for several more hours, deliberately leaving the office door open. A number of the inmates wandered in, each on some outrageous pretext. Kane would watch and listen and soothe. Fell poked his head in once, but waved and went away when he saw that Reno was there: the inmate had asked for Kane's opinion on whether two Pekingese "would look ridiculous" as Rosencrantz and Guildenstern.

After dinner, Kane roamed the mansion's main hall for a time, seemingly encouraging the inmates to approach him. He checked some new paintings on the easels. He waited. But Cutshaw did not appear. At ten, Kane went up to his bedroom and began to prepare himself for sleep. But there were constant visitors barging through his door, inmates with problems and with grievances. The last of them were Fromme and an inmate named Price.

"May I speak to you for a moment?" Fromme asked him, standing at the door.

"Of course."

"I want schooling, sir. May I have it? I want to fulfill my life's ambition. When I get out of here, of course. But I just can't live without my dream, sir. It's been my dream since I was a boy. I'm thirty-five, but it isn't too late if I go to school. Could I go right away? Maybe 'Operation Bootstrap,' Colonel?"

Kane asked him what level of schooling he had completed and whether his credits would be sufficient to admit him to medical school.

"Medical school?" Fromme blinked. "No. I want to play the violin. I want to play like John Garfield in *Humoresque*. I want to play that scene. I want people to think I'm just a kid from the slums, and then, zappo! I whip out the violin and I stun Joan Crawford and her snotty rich friends. I want to play that scene all the time."

Kane was kind.

Price was more difficult. A wiry, blond-haired man with deep-set eyes that probed like death rays out of a gaunt and cadaverous face, he bulled his way into the bedroom.

"I want my flying belt," he demanded.

"I beg your pardon?"

Price looked away in disgust. "Yeah, yeah, same act, same old routine. Christ!" He turned back to Kane and began to speak in the manner of a man repressing frustration and terrible anger, his voice growing louder and more belligerent as he spoke. "Yeah, I want my flying belt, okay? Yeah, sure, you've never heard of it. Right? *Bullshit!* Now kindly have the goodness to admit that you're able to read my thoughts! that my spaceship has crashed on the planet Venus! that this *is* Venus and you're a Venusian and that you've illegally invaded my mind to try to make me believe that I'm still on earth! I'm not on earth and you're not an earthman! I'm standing here up to my asshole in fungus," Price shouted, "and you're a giant *brain!*" He abruptly assumed a conciliatory tone: "Come on, now, give me back my flying belt; I won't use it to escape, I swear it!"

Kane asked him why he wanted the belt and Price reverted to acid hostility. "I want to play Tinker Bell in drag in a fungoid production of *Peter Pan*. All right? Are you happy? Now, where the hell is it?"

"It's coming," Kane said softly.

"But why is it *gone?*" Price asked. Then he leaned his head conspiratorially, whispering, "Listen! The brain named Cutshaw says you're not a brain at all. He said that your name is Sibylline Books. Is that the truth?"

"No."

"Dammit, who can I *believe!*" bawled Price. He lowered his voice. "Listen, he offered me a deal. He said if I gave him the map coordinates of the factory on my planet that manufactures all those CB radios, he'd get me back the belt. He wants to bomb the fucking factory. But I was loyal. Understand? I told him no, that you'd feel hurt. Now let's reciprocate, you bastard!" Again Price's voice was loud and shrill. "Help me out or I might find a way to *kill* you, to give you ultimate migraine headache! Where's the *belt!*"

"We'll have one soon."

"What the hell do you take me for, a stupe? Why the Christ do you think my government picked me? Because I see real good in space? I've had all the crap and hocus-pocus I can take! Understand? Produce the belt in twenty-four hours or you're in trouble! Now go and wrap yourself in fronds or whatever you do when you have to sleep! I am sealing off my mind!"

Price's departure left Kane exhausted. He lay down on his bed and covered his eyes with the crook of his arm. And he was suddenly deeply asleep and dreaming: Rain. The jungle. The man with the Z-shaped scar on his brow. Kane was kneeling by a body again, the Franciscan. And someone was hunting him, coming closer and closer each second. The man with the scar was looking down at him. He looked at his hands: they were holding the ends of a bloodstained wire. "Colonel let's get out of here, let's get out of here, let's get—"

Abruptly the dream was penetrated by someone's scream of agony, and Kane found himself jerking bolt upright, awake. He felt a confusion. Someone needed him. He realized with a start that it was morning. He closed his eyes again. There was a light rapping at the door. He stood up wearily and went to answer it, expecting to find an inmate. It was Fell.

"Come on in," said Kane.

Fell entered.

"What's wrong?" asked Kane.

"Wrong?"

"Yes, what is it? Can I help?"

Fell scrutinized him intently, then shook his head and sat down in an overstuffed chair near the bed. "No, nothing's wrong. I just thought I'd check in with you, see how you were doing."

Kane sat on the edge of the bed near Fell. Fell was wearing a khaki shirt and pants. He lit a cigarette. Fanning out the match, he peered across at Kane. "Jesus, you look beat. Didn't you sleep?"

"Not till late. There was always an inmate at the door with some problem."

"Then keep the door locked," said Fell.

"No," said Kane vehemently. "They've got to be able to see me whenever they need to."

"Hey, look, can I tell you something?" said Fell. "I've got a suspicion these constant bangings on your door are just part of a plan to convince you that they're sick and that it's all for real. And I want you to notice something: these guys did the same thing to me my first day here; and then it slackened off—until you got here. Then it started all over again with you."

"I see the point," murmured Kane. "Yes, I see."

"Cutshaw's their leader, the goddam mastermind; in a word, the biggest pain in the ass. Anyway, that's how I see it; you can take it for what it's worth. You want breakfast?"

"What?" Kane looked dazed.

"Do you want any breakfast?"

Kane seemed far away. He was staring out the window. It was raining very heavily again. The sky was dark and distant thunder rumbled and crackled. He shut his eyes and put his head down, pinching the corners of his eyes with thumb and finger.

"Something wrong?" asked Fell.

Kane shook his head.

"Something right?"

"That dream," Kane murmured.

"What was that?"

"I just flashed on a dream I keep having. A nightmare."

Fell raised his feet and plopped them onto a hassock. "As Calpurnia said to Sigmund Freud, you tell me your dream and I'll tell you mine."

"It isn't my dream," said Kane.

"Beg pardon?"

"I said it isn't my dream." Kane spoke softly. "A patient of mine—a former patient: a colonel just back from Vietnam—he had a grotesque recurring nightmare. It was something that happened to him in combat; or at least the central idea of it was. And ever since he told me about it . . ." Kane paused; and then he turned haunted eyes on Fell. "Ever since he told me about it," he repeated, "*I* keep dreaming it."

"Jesus," breathed Fell.

"Yes. Exactly." Kane looked away. "It's very strange."

" 'Strange' isn't the word. I mean, isn't that carrying transference just a little bit far?"

Kane looked at him a moment before he answered. "I suppose it's all right to tell you this now." He looked down at the rug on the floor. "Yes. At this point, why not? It was my brother."

"The patient?"

"Yes."

"Aha. *Twin* brother?"

"No."

"Well, that still would tend to explain it, though," said Fell. "You're psychically attuned. You're brothers. You're very close."

"No, we're not."

"But you must be."

"Fell, have you ever heard of 'Killer' Kane?" Kane was now looking straight into Fell's eyes.

"Buck Rogers," grunted Fell.

"No, not that 'Killer' Kane: 'Killer' Kane the Marine."

"Oh, well, sure. Who hasn't? The guerrilla-warfare

guy. Killed forty, fifty men with his hands. Or was it eighty? Hey, hold it! Are you saying . . .?"

"That's my brother," said Kane.

"You're kidding!"

Kane shook his head.

"You're *kidding!*" Fell was sitting up straight, his expression at once amazed and pleased.

Kane looked away. "I wish I were."

"*Uh*-oh; do I detect that you don't get along?"

"You do."

"When you were kids he put frogs in your bed at night. Is that it? Here, lie down and free-associate," Fell said wryly. "Talk about your brother."

"He's a killer," said Kane.

"He's a Marine. He gets dropped behind enemy lines and does his duty. Jesus, you're serious about this." Fell frowned. "Come on, man, he's a hero." Then, "Aha!" he pounced. "Sibling rivalry!"

Kane said, "Let's forget it."

"Are you sure you know what business you're in? These recruiting-office sergeants can be sneaky."

Kane closed his eyes and held his hand out to Fell, palm outward, in a gesture suggesting that Fell desist.

"You a friend of Jane Fonda?" pressed Fell.

"We're close."

"You're kidding."

"I'm kidding."

Fell nodded and stood up. "I'm for coffee. You coming?"

Kane stayed seated. "In a minute or two. I need to change."

"Yeah, sure. How's your brother, by the way? You know, I met him when I was stationed in Korea. That was quite a little while ago, but I remember him. A hell of a guy. We palled around. I really liked him. I liked him very much, in fact."

"He's dead," said Kane.

"Oh, Jesus. Hey, I'm sorry. I really am sorry."

"That's all right. That's why I told you about the dream."

Fell looked despondent. "Listen, how did it—" He stopped. "Never mind." He opened the door and pointed down. "See you downstairs," he said.

Kane nodded.

Fell closed the door behind him and fumbled for a cigarette with trembling fingers. Tears coursed down his face.

Stripped to the waist, Kane sat on the edge of the examination table in the clinic. Fell continued with the physical checkup Kane had submitted to at his nagging insistence.

"Any blurring of the vision? Any feeling of just generally seeming unglued?"

"No."

Fell grunted and shone a penlight into Kane's eyes. Then he clicked it off and slipped it into a pocket of his white jacket. Folding his arms, he leaned back against a wall and looked up at Kane. "If you don't take to locking your bedroom door at night and scheduling regular office hours for consultation with the inmates, I'm recommending Rest and Reassignment, Doctor, and it won't take long to process, believe me. I've got all kinds of juice where it counts."

Over the past ten days the inmates, especially Cutshaw, had subjected Kane to barrages and sallies by day and by night.

"I'm serious," said Fell. "You're just plain driving

yourself too hard. On the level. I can do that. You want that done? Reassignment?"

Kane's eyebrows knitted together. "What's wrong with me?"

"Chronic fatigue, for one thing. Rapid pulse rate. Your blood pressure's fine for an attacking rhino. What the hell are you trying to prove?"

Kane lowered his head and was silent. Then he murmured, "Maybe so."

"Maybe what?"

"We might do with a few restrictions. A couple. I'll think about it."

"Hooray. Now you're getting some sense."

Neither man could see Cutshaw eavesdropping out in the hall, a little to the side of the open clinic door. Hearing footsteps coming down the stairs, Cutshaw hurried away, pale and troubled.

"Picking up any insights?" asked Fell. "Any answers?"

Kane slipped his shirt off a hanger on a tree pole. "Maybe Cutshaw," he said, looking thoughtful.

"What about him?"

"He keeps after me on God, on metaphysical questions." He slipped on the shirt and began to button it. "There are some of us who feel that the root of all neuroses lies in the failure of an individual to perceive any meaning in his life, or in the universe. A religious experience is the answer to that."

"That's what Cutshaw wants? Religion?"

"He wants his father to be Albert Einstein and Albert Einstein to believe in God."

"Then the men aren't faking it. Is that what you believe? I mean, is that your instinct?"

Kane said simply, "I don't know."

They left it at that.

The following day, Kane was standing in the hall alone, examining a painting by one of the inmates, when Fell came up beside him. "How's the boy?"

"I'm fine," said Kane, his eyes still fixed on the

painting. It was the one with the needle through the finger.

Fell gestured at it with a move of his head. "Does that mean something?"

"All of them do. They're clues to a man's unconscious. Like dreams."

Fell lit a cigarette. "And what about *your* dream?" he asked. "Still having it?"

Kane did not respond. Instead he said, "Cutshaw doesn't paint. That's too bad." He looked thoughtfully at Fell. He studied him intently. A troubled look had furrowed the skin around his eyes. "I dreamed about *you* last night," he said.

"Really? What did you dream?"

"I don't remember," said Kane, still troubled. "It was something odd."

The men looked up at the sound of barking.

"Colonel!"

Reno and his dog bounded up to them. Breathlessly, Reno said, "Colonel, I'm in trouble. You've got to help me."

Fell said, "Take an enema and check with my service tomorrow morning."

Reno cupped his hands around his mouth so that his voice took on a boomy resonance. "Dr. Fell, you're wanted in surgery. Put some acupuncture needles where you need them most." He glared at Fell and muttered, "Jerk!" Then he turned to Kane. "I meant motivational trouble, not medical. I speak of the problem of Hamlet's madness. I've been having an argument, Colonel, a monster, and I'd like you to settle it once and for all." Reno frowned. His dog sat on its haunches beside him. "Listen, here's the puzzlement, the perplexity, the curious, mysterious fandango. Do you mind if I sit down, by the way?"

"Go ahead," said Kane.

Reno sat on the floor. "Now, some—" He broke off and glared at Fell, who was laughing, a hand pressed over his mouth. Reno said blackly, "Why don't you go inoculate a fucking armadillo, Fell. Get lost, pal. Take a hike."

"Let's go into my office," said Kane.

"Yeah, sure."

As they walked with him, Kane prodded him gently. "You were saying?"

"Lovely man. I was saying that some Shakespearean scholars say that when Hamlet's pretending he's crazy, he really *is* crazy. Correct?"

Kane turned to look at Reno. "That's so," he said.

"But other Shakespearean scholars say that when Hamlet's pretending he's nuts, he really *isn't* nuts. They say it's an act. Now, Colonel, I come to you as a shrinker and as a sympathetic pussycat. Please give me *your* opinion."

"I'd like to hear yours first," said Kane.

"Terrific psychiatrist! That's class!"

They had arrived at the office. Kane stood and Fell sat down on the sofa. Reno stood near the door with his dog.

"Okay, now," said Reno, "let's look at what Hamlet does. First, he *shtravanses* around the place in his underwear. Correct? And that's only for openers." Reno started ticking off the points on his fingers. "Then he calls the king his mother; tells a nice old man, a hard worker, that he's senile; he throws a tantrum at a theater party; and then he starts talking dirty to his girlfriend while she's sitting there watching the play. She just came there to *watch* it; what did she come there for, to hear Hamlet's dirty mouth?"

Kane began to speak, but Reno interrupted.

"Like a sewer, Hamlet's mouth! Good God almighty, that's his girlfriend there!"

"Ophelia," grunted Fell, blowing smoke.

"Very nice," grated Reno. "So much for your medical confidentiality."

"The problem," urged Kane.

"Yes, the problem. The problem is this. Pay attention! Considering how Hamlet is acting, is he really and truly nuts?"

Kane said, "Yes," as Fell was saying, "No."

Reno said, *"Both* of you are wrong!"

Kane and Fell looked at each other without expression. Reno ran to Kane's desk and leaped up on it, sitting on its edge. He lectured Kane and Fell. "Take a look at what happens: his father dies; his girl leaves him *flat;* then comes an appearance by his father's ghost. Bad enough, but then the ghost says he was murdered. And by whom? By Hamlet's uncle! Who recently married Hamlet's *mother!* Listen, that by *itself* is a great big hangup; Hamlet, he *liked* his mother—a *lot!* Listen, never mind that: I don't want to talk *filth.* All I say is, what happens to this poor schmuck is very unsettling at the *least.* And when you see he's a sensitive, high-strung kid, all these things are enough to drive him crazy. And that's especially when you consider all of this happened in very cold weather."

"Then Hamlet's insane," Kane concluded.

"No, he isn't," corrected Reno, his face glowing. "He *is* pretending. But—*but!*—if he hadn't pretended to be crazy, he *would* have gone crazy!"

Kane's demeanor grew more intensely alert. He kept his gaze locked firmly on Reno.

"See, Hamlet isn't psycho," the inmate continued. "However, he's hanging on the brink. A little push, you know, an eensy little teensy little shove, and the kid would be gone! Bananas! Whacked out! And Hamlet knows this! Not his conscious mind: *un*consciously he knows it; so his unconscious makes him do what keeps him sane: namely, acting like he's nuts! 'Cause acting nutty is a safety valve, a way to let off steam; a way to get rid of your fucking aggressions and all of your guilts and your fears and your—"

Fell started to interrupt and Reno cut him off sharply, warning, "Watch, you! Don't talk dirty!"

"I never talk—"

"Quiet, you! I know you: a dirty mind in a dirty clinic! Even your dental floss is dirty!"

Avidly, Reno turned back to Kane. "Little Booboo, Hamlet *avoids* going crazy by *pretending* that he's crazy; by doing ridiculous, terrible things. And the crazier he acts, the *healthier* he gets!"

"Yes," breathed Kane. There was dawning in his eyes.

"I mean terrible," Reno continued. "But meantime, he's safe; understand me? Look, if I did what Hamlet does in the play, they'd lock me up, you understand? They'd put me away in an institution. But him? Prince Royal Garbagemouth? *He* gets away with murder. And why? Because *nuts are not responsible for their actions!*"

"Yes!" Kane was agitated.

"Does *Hamlet* think he's crazy?" asked Fell.

"Come on, nobody crazy thinks he's crazy," Reno answered disdainfully. "Christ, what a *putz*."

Neither Kane nor Fell spoke. Reno said, "Does silence mean consent?"

"*A Man for All Seasons,*" murmured Fell.

Reno shook his head in disbelief.

Kane's eyes were fevered. "I think," he told Reno, "I agree with your theory."

Triumphantly, Reno whirled on his dog. "There! You *see,* dumb, stubborn idiot! From now on we do the scene *my* way!" He turned to Kane, said, "God bless your arteries, Colonel," and walked out of the office. "Come on," he snapped at the dog. "Rip Torn, you don't know shit!"

Kane sat down at his desk and stared at his telephone. After a silence, Fell spoke. "I want you to listen to me," he said. "Groper laid on some rules today, like no more visitations with you after seven o'—"

"Groper shouldn't have done that!" Kane interrupted.

"*I* told him to do it."

"You had no right!"

"I told you, you're driving youself too hard!" Fell's voice was heated.

"I want the restrictions lifted," said Kane.

"Terrific!" Fell shook his head. "I'll bet dollars to

doughnuts that the Hamlet theory is a ploy dreamed up by Cutshaw to *get* you to lift the restrictions."

Kane's face was alive, excited.

"Any comment on that, Little Booboo?" asked Fell.

"I only wish," Kane said fervently, "I were sure that it was so!"

"Oh, you can be sure, all right. Take a look in Cutshaw's footlocker and you'll find a book called *Madness in Hamlet*. You know what's in it? The theory that Reno just gave us."

"You're *sure?*"

"I'm sure."

"So Cutshaw put Reno up to it!"

"What else?"

"Good! It fits!" said Kane.

"The hole in my head?"

"The Hamlet theory is correct: it's precisely the condition of most of these men! And Cutshaw's sending in Reno to explain it is just like those paintings out there in the hall: someone's disguised and terrified shout for us to help him—and *telling us how!*"

"And that someone is Cutshaw?"

"His unconscious!"

Kane picked up the telephone receiver and pressed on the intercom buzzer. Then he gazed up at Fell. "Incidentally, how do you know what's in Cutshaw's footlocker?"

"Can't tell you. 'Medical confidentiality.' "

"Get me Fort Lewis," Kane ordered into the phone. He sounded exhilarated. "Quartermaster's Office. Thank you." Kane hung up and awaited the connection.

"What are you doing?" Fell asked.

"We're going to need some supplies."

"What for?"

"We are going to give the men their 'safety valve' to the greatest possible degree. We are going to indulge them monumentally."

"Precisely how do you propose to do that?" Fell asked.

Kane explained it.

Fell looked troubled. "Do it in writing," he advised. "Don't you think?"

"Oh?"

"It's a little far out for most people, not to speak of the military mind," reasoned Fell. "If I were you, I'd lay the arguments out on paper."

"You think so."

"Give the imbeciles something to look at. Pieces of paper make them feel more secure."

Kane thought. Then he buzzed and canceled the call, and Cutshaw burst in upon them, exclaiming. "We want to play *Great Escape!*" He pounded a fist on Kane's desk. "We want shovels, picks and jackhammers!"

Fell decided that Cutshaw must have been eavesdropping in the hall outside the office while Kane was explaining his new approach. He excused himself, went to his bedroom, telephoned the Pentagon general again and had an argument. He lost. That evening he flew to Washington and early the next day he resumed the argument in person. This time he won.

On his return, Kane asked where he'd been.

"Got an uncle in trouble," Fell explained.

"Can I help?"

"You're helping. Every kind thought is the hope of the world."

Major Groper held on to the railing of the second-story balustrade and looked incredulously at a scaffold bearing Gomez as it creaked slowly upward toward the ceiling. On his way to "paint the ceiling like the Sistine Chapel," Gomez was stirring one of several large buckets of paint.

He hove up close to the adjutant. "Some weather," said Gomez.

Groper said, *"Jesus Christ almighty!"*

He looked below. A pack of dogs of various breeds were yapping, barking and howling outside a utility room that faced on the main hall. Krebs held their tethers. Groper saw Kane emerge from his office and walk over to the sergeant. The door to the utility room flew open, disclosing an agitated Reno. Looking into the room, he commanded, "Out! Get out! Take a walk!" A large chow padded out of the utility room, and Reno called after him acidly, "Tell your stupid agent never to waste any more of my time!"

Reno saw Kane and approached him, outraged. "Can

85

you imagine?" he said. "He *lisps!* Here I am casting
Julius Caesar and the idiots send me a dog that *lisps!*"
He turned and called back into the utility room. "You
too, Nammack! Get lost!"

Out came Nammack, clad in a brand-new blue-and-
red Superman costume. "But why?" asked Nammack.
"Tell me *why!* Just give me one reason that makes any
—"

Reno interrupted, exasperated. "Colonel Kane,
would you do me a favor? Please? Would you kindly
explain to this imbecile here that in none of the plays
of Shakespeare can there be a part for Superman?"

"There could be, the way I explained it," Nammack
sulked.

"The way you ex*plained* it!" Incredulous, Reno
whirled on Kane. "You know what he wants? You want
to hear? When the conspirators draw their knives, he
wants to *rescue* Julius Caesar! Honest to God! He
wants to swoop down like a rocket, pick him up and
then go hurdling mighty temples at a single, incredible
bound! He—"

Paint splattered down in gobs, and Reno looked up
and saw Gomez. "Fucking bananas," he murmured.
"*Bananas!*" Reno told the sergeant, "Next!" and Krebs
released the leash of an eager Afghan. Reno escorted it
into the room. "You bring any photographs with you?"
he asked as he closed the door.

Price appeared before them. He was encased in a
NASA spacesuit, a simulated flying belt on his back. He
spoke through a miniature loudspeaker system built into the suit. "Any news from Earth?" he asked Kane in
a voice that resonated electronically. He turned down
the volume. "Sorry. Any letters?"

"Your planet has demanded your return," said Kane.

"Fuck that. Any packages? When I was on Mars my
mother sent a cheesecake every month. She used to
pack it in popcorn to keep it moist. All that shit about
canals on Mars is a myth. Take my word, Mars is
drier than an asshole in hell."

Outside, an ambulance siren wailed; Fromme was

driving it around the grounds, testing the equipment. He now wore a stethoscope of his own and had a surgeon's gown and medical bag.

"Yes, Mars is dry," said Kane.

"Nice fungus you got there. Moist. I like things moist."

"I'll check on the cheesecake," said Kane.

"Giant Brain, you're okay," said Price. "I'd shake your hand, but I can't make the scene with the tentacles. Jesus, I can't even eat calamary. Oh, excuse me. I'm sorry. I didn't mean to offend you."

"No offense."

"You never know what might piss people off on different planets. Once on Uranus I said 'tomato,' and I was in jail so goddam fast it made my head swim. The Earth ambassador had to spring me. People are touchy. You brains wear clothes? Never mind. Don't answer. I don't want to know. Tabu. That's a perfume back on Earth. You know what? I'll tell you: this place is nice."

Groper watched and listened in a daze. From outside on the grounds, he heard Fromme honking the ambulance horn at Fairbanks, who was dressed like Steve McQueen in *The Great Escape* and was zooming about on a motorcycle. He saw Kane walk slowly to a cellar door. When he opened it, the shattering sound of a jackhammer ripped at the naked air from below, where Cutshaw and most of the other inmates had embarked upon a tunneling operation.

In the basement, Cutshaw yelled, "Cut that thing off for a minute!"

"Yeah, okay." An inmate turned off the jackhammer. A loud, creamy hush enveloped the group.

"Now then, notice," said Cutshaw. He was lecturing some men who were gathered before him. With a wooden pointer he tapped a blueprint tacked to an easel. "Tunnel One and Tunnel Two are decoys. Three is the big one. Three is a maximum security."

"Where does it go, Big X?" asked a redheaded inmate named Caponegro.

The astronaut beamed. "My son, it goes absolutely

nowhere. Incidentally, these tunnels are strictly out of bounds for Reno. If you see him here, chase him immediately; there'll be slippage enough as it is, without his fucking dogs down here. Let's be sure that he's—"

Cutshaw broke off as he noticed Kane looking down from the doorway at the top of the stairs. "Heavenly caribou, you are ours!" he shouted up joyously. "Ours alone and no one else's!" The men began cheering and applauding.

Groper could not bear it any longer. "Jesus!" he croaked. "Jesus Christ!" He looked down at his hands. They were squeezing the railing and his knuckles were white.

Groper went searching for Colonel Fell. When he found him in the clinic, Groper was shaking. Fell was at his desk, talking quietly to Krebs, who was sitting on the edge of the examining table.

"What the hell is *happening?*" the adjutant cried out, his voice on the verge of cracking. "This is *crazy!* For Christ's sake, Fell, what's going *on?* Do you know they're digging tunnels downstairs in the basement? They're fucking *digging* down there! They've got a jackhammer!"

"Oh, well, how far can they get?" said Fell. He had a drink in his hand.

"That isn't the point!" shouted Groper.

"What is?"

"This whole thing is *crazy!*"

Groper had entered the service as a volunteer at the age of eighteen. For a man from a slum background, the service meant escape from the constant indignities of poverty. Groper had read and reread *Beau Geste,* and in the Marines he had expected a life of pursuing the "Blue Water," a self-esteem based on honor and valor and romantic ideals. The bizarre goings-on at the mansion and his partial custodianship were the ultimate attack on whatever he valued in himself. "Kane should be stopped! For Chrissakes, he doesn't know what the hell he's doing! He doesn't know *shit* about the service! I checked in his 201 file: he's a goddam dumb civilian;

he got a stupid direct commission just six months ago! What in the hell is he doing in command? What the hell is he *doing!*"

"He's got an idea that if he indulges all the fantasies of these men, it'll prove an accelerated catharsis for them. In other words, they'll be cured."

"But that's preposterous!"

"You got any better ideas?"

"But these guys aren't sick; they're all faking!"

"Oh, fuck you, Groper."

Groper's broad veined nostrils flared. He darted a glance at the cup in Fell's hand. "You're drunk," he said.

Sergeant Christian came into the room. He was carrying a stack of cardboard clothing boxes. He put one of them on the examining table. "Your uniform, sir," he told Fell. "They just came in." Then he looked at Groper. "Sir, I put yours in your office. On your desk."

"*What* uniform?"

No one answered.

Later that evening, Groper stormed into Kane's office. Kane was at his desk, staring out at the rain. He did not turn at Groper's entrance.

Groper was breathless. "Sir, why do I have to wear this?" he demanded.

Kane turned slowly and looked at the adjutant. Groper was dressed in a German Gestapo uniform from the era of World War II. So was Kane. "What?" asked the colonel. His stare was numb and remote, and he winced as if in pain. A trembling hand traveled slowly to his forehead. He seemed displaced, uncomprehending. "What did you say?" he repeated.

"I said, why do I have to wear this?"

Kane jerked his head slightly, as if he was clearing a blurring of his vision. "It's called psychodrama, Major. It's a more or less accepted tool of therapy. The inmates are playing the role of Allied prisoners of war attempting to tunnel their way to freedom." Kane appeared to be squinting now. "We are their captors," he said.

"We're their *prisoners!*" Groper cried angrily. His new-found knowledge that Kane had no military background, and was therefore a civilian in Groper's eyes, had freed the adjutant of his former inexplicable fear. "Nothing but yellow-bellied goof-offs have a ball out there!" he blurted. "I mean, Christ! Why do *I* have to help their fun? *I'm* not a psychiatrist! I'm a *Marine!* By God, it's an unfair imposition and I think I've got a right to—"

He broke off and took a step backward. Seething, shaking, Kane rose and cut him off in an icy, hoarsely whispered voice that gathered fury with every word: "Jesus! Jesus *Christ*, man! Why don't you love somebody a little! Why don't you *help* somebody a little! Help them! Help! For the love of Christ! You green-soaked, caterpillar-torturing bastard, you're going to wear that uniform, bathe in it, sleep in it. Try to take it off and you'll *die* in it! *Is that clear!*" Kane leaned over the desk, his weight supported on trembling fingertips.

Groper's eyes were wide. He backpedaled slowly toward the door. "Yes, sir." He was stunned. Behind him, the door flew open and knocked him to the floor. Cutshaw slipped in, looked at Groper, snatched the American flag from the wall and placed a foot on the major's neck, announcing, "I claim this swamp for Poland!"

"Groper, get out of here!" Kane said shakily.

"Immediately!" added Cutshaw as the adjutant knocked away the flag and quickly scrambled to his feet. "And keep that uniform clean," added Cutshaw. "I'm putting you in for Best of Show."

Groper averted his eyes and left. Cutshaw stared after him for a moment; then he turned to Kane. "What's up? What's going on?"

Kane was at his desk again. His head was propped in his hands. "Nothing," he said. He looked up at Cutshaw. Compassion pooled in his eyes. "What is it?" he asked gently. "What can I do for you?"

"Well, for one thing, Major Strasser, my men want

proper toilet facilities every fifty feet of tunnel. Can you provide that?"

"Yes," said Kane.

Cutshaw glanced swiftly at the wall he had once attempted to climb. "Incidentally, have you fixed that goddam wall yet?"

"No."

"But you'll *fix* it."

"Yes."

"Who are you?"

Kane's face was in shadow. He did not reply.

"Who are you?" Cutshaw repeated. "You're too human to be human." His face turned suspicious. He walked to the desk. "I'd like a sucker," he told Kane grimly.

"What?"

"A sucker, a common lollipop. Can I have one?"

"Why?"

"Okay; so you're not Pat O'Brien. Pat O'Brien would have given me a sucker without putting me through a third degree or checking my fucking credit references. Who the hell are you? All this suspense is a pain in the ass. Maybe you're P. T. Barnum," he ventured. "P. T. Barnum slaughtered lambs. He set up this cage at his side show, see, and he stuck in a panther and a lamb together. And there was never any trouble. Huddy, the public just went wild! They said, 'Lookit, a panther and a lamb and they don't even argue! They don't even *discuss!*' But, Hud, what the public never knew was that it was never the same poor lamb. That fucking panther ate up a lamb every single day at intermission for three hundred days, and then they shot him for asking for mint sauce. Animals are innocent. Why should they suffer?"

"Why should men?"

"Ah, come on, that's a setup; that you've got answers for. Like pain makes people noble and how could a man be more than a talking, chess-playing panda bear if there weren't at least the *possibility* of suffering. But what about animals, Hud? Does pain make turkeys noble? Why is all of creation based on dog eat dog, and the little fish are eaten by the big fish, animals screaming in pain, all creation an open wound, a fucking slaughterhouse?"

"Maybe things weren't like that at first."

"Oh, really?"

"Maybe 'Original Sin' is just a metaphor for some horrible genetic mutation in all living things a long, long time ago. Maybe we caused those mutations somehow: a nuclear war that involved the whole planet, perhaps. I don't know. But perhaps that's what we mean by the 'Fall'; and why innocent babies could be said to have inherited Adam's sin. Genetics. We're mutations; monsters, if you will."

"Then why doesn't Foot just *tell* us that? Why in Christ can't he simply make an appearance on top of the Empire State Building and give us the word? Then we'd all be good! What the fuck is the problem? Is Foot running short on tablets of stone? My Uncle Eddie owns a quarry; I can get them for him wholesale."

"You're asking for miracles," Kane observed.

"I'm asking for Foot to either shit or get off the pot! Diarrhetic strange gods have been waiting in line!"

"But—"

"A busload of orphans went over a cliff today! I heard it on the news."

"Maybe God can't interfere in our affairs."

"Yes, so I've noticed." Cutshaw sat down on the couch.

"Maybe God can't interfere because to do so would spoil his plan for something in the future," Kane appealed. There was a caring in his voice and his eyes. "Some evolution of man and the world," he continued, "that's so unimaginably beautiful that it's worth all the tears and all the pain of every suffering thing that ever lived; and maybe when we get to that moment in time we'll look back and say, 'Yes; yes, I'm glad that it was so!' "

"I say it's spinach and to hell with it."

Kane leaned forward. "You're convinced that God is dead because of the evil in the world?"

"Correct."

"Then why don't you think he's *alive* because of the goodness in the world?"

"What goodness?"

"Everywhere! It's all around us!"

"After an answer so zestfully fatuous, I feel I should terminate this discussion."

"If we're nothing but atoms, just molecular structures no different in kind from this desk or this pen, then how is it there is love in this world? I mean love as a God might love. How is it that a man will give his life for another?"

"Never happened," said Cutshaw.

"Of course it's happened. It happens all the time." Kane was not reasoning dispassionately: he was arguing, involved.

"Give me one example," Cutshaw demanded.

"But it's obviously true."

"*Give me one example!*" Cutshaw was up and had marched to the desk, confronting Kane.

"A soldier throws himself on top of a live grenade to prevent the other men in his squad from being hit."

"That's reflex action," Cutshaw snapped.

"But—"

"Prove that it isn't!"

Kane looked down and examined his thoughts. Then he looked up at Cutshaw and said, "All right. A shipwreck survivor in the middle of the ocean finds out that she has meningitis and deliberately goes over the side of the lifeboat, drowning herself to keep the others in the boat from contracting the disease. Now, what do you call that? Reflex action?"

"No, I call that suicide."

"Suicide and giving up your life are not the same."

"You're so dumb you're adorable."

"The essence of suicide is despair."

"The essence of suicide," Cutshaw rebutted, "is nobody gets to collect the insurance." Kane started to reply, but Cutshaw argued over his voice: "All the examples you're trying to give me or are going to give me can be explained."

"Like the way you explained that woman in the lifeboat?"

"She might have had children in that lifeboat, which makes her performance maternal instinct. Maybe somebody pushed her over the side."

"Not so," said Kane with a shake of his head.

"How the hell do *you* know? Were you there?"

"No, of course not; it's just an example."

"Right! That's exactly my point! That's what I'm getting at: Who the hell knows whether all the examples we keep on hearing about aren't bullshit, or don't have some bullshit, basically selfish explanation?"

"*I* know," Kane asserted firmly.

"I don't! Now give me one—just one—example that you know of *personally!*"

Kane was silent, his eyes on Cutshaw's, burning, mysterious.

"Just one! That guy with the grenade, maybe?"

Kane stared down at the desk.

Cutshaw's tone became forlorn. "I thought as much," he muttered. Then quickly he was animated, manic. "Tomorrow's Sunday," he announced. "I want you to take me to Mass."

"But your God is dead," said Kane.

"That's right. But I have a deep and trenchant interest in the study of primitive cults. Besides, I love to worship statues just as long as I don't have to look at their feet. Have you ever seen anything as tawdry as the feet of an old St. Joseph statue with the faded paint and the crummy old plaster chipped away on the toes? You want to talk about sleazy? Holy *Christ!* Listen, take me to Mass tomorrow. I'm serious. I'll be quiet and good, Hud, I swear it. Please? I'll just sit and think pious thoughts. Okay?"

Kane was silent, considering.

"Okay, fronds? Can I think about fronds? Or I'll sit there and quietly think about pianos!" He leaned his

face in close to Kane's. "I want to go," he said softly. "Really."

Kane agreed to take him. Cutshaw loped from the
room, euphoric. He ran out to the courtyard, clapping
his arms around his chest as a chilling breeze sprang
up and the vivid orange ball of the sun slipped down
below the tree line into darkness. Groper stood at his
office window, watching him. He saw Krebs and Chris-
tain enter the courtyard. The two sergeants were
dressed in Nazi Storm Trooper uniforms, each with a
rifle slung over his shoulder and a German shepherd in
tow. They took up positions a distance apart at the
outer perimeter of the yard and began pacing off a sentry watch. When Cutshaw saw them he let out a yip-
ping cheer. Groper shook his head. He would check
Kane's file again. He remembered a paragraph dealing
with his psychiatric methods. A word eluded him. Was
it "novel"? "Erratic"? He asked a clerk-typist to
dig out the file, and to put in another tracer on Fell's,
which had never arrived. He shuffled the papers on his
desk and noted that a new inmate was due to arrive. He
buzzed for an orderly and told him to get a bed ready.

Krebs and Christian patrolled until eleven, when the
lights were turned out. Once, earlier, they had approached each other from opposite ends of the courtyard and halted briefly at close quarters and Krebs
had intoned, "I'll bet my savage dog can lick *your*
savage dog." Christian refused to be lured into answering, and the sergeants continued walking and were
never observed to converse again the entire evening.

The following morning just before seven, Kane sat
waiting in his staff car, having sent Krebs to go and
fetch Cutshaw. When the astronaut finally appeared,
he was dressed in a clean khaki uniform, stiff with
starch. His hair was thick with Vaseline and his face
was cleanly shaven, but he still wore his sneakers and
his tattered college blazer, and affected a bold, high
Buster Brown collar tied with a bright-red bow. Kane
at first insisted that he remove the collar and sneakers,
but relented when Cutshaw argued, "Would Foot give

a shit about what I'm wearing?" They drove to the church, a modest A-frame in the seacoast town of Bly. They were a few minutes late.

As they emerged from the staff car, Cutshaw looked suddenly terrified and gripped Kane's hand. He would not let go until after they had entered the church.

In the vestibule, Kane stopped to dip his hand into the holy-water font, and Cutshaw walked rapidly toward the front of the church, assuming a rapid, pigeon-toed gait and listing his shoulders from side to side. When he reached the front pew he paused and called to Kane in a loud stage whisper, "Hud, up here! Let's see the statues!"

Kane walked down the aisle, ignoring the curious looks of the parishioners. He genuflected outside the pew, then rose and knelt down next to Cutshaw. The astronut was kneeling stiffly, staring piously at the priest, whose hands were upraised, his back to the parishioners. "Is that Edgar Cayce?" he asked in a voice that carried to the altar. The priest paused briefly and looked around, then resumed the saying of Mass.

Cutshaw was quiet until the sermon, which concerned the Good Shepherd who was willing to "lay down his life for his sheep." Whenever the priest made some trenchant point, Cutshaw applauded or murmured "Bravo!" The priest, a former missionary who had lived much of his life in China, decided that Cutshaw was drunk and certainly no more of a nuisance than squalling infants or belching warlords. When Cutshaw applauded he would raise his voice a notch and offer it up to God.

When it came time for the collection, Cutshaw loudly demanded a nickel. Kane gave him a dollar. But when the collection basket was thrust at him, Cutshaw held it firmly and poked his nose in it, sniffing furiously; then he abruptly waved it by. He crumpled the dollar into his pocket.

Kane turned his gaze to him as they knelt for the consecration. Cutshaw's hands were clasped before him as he stared up at the altar, his pixie head awash in sunlight shafting narrowly through stained glass. He looked like a Christmas-card sketch of a choirboy.

Cutshaw behaved with decorum through the remaining parts of the Mass, except once, when he stood up and said, "Infinite goodness is creating a being that you know in advance is going to complain."

As they walked back up the aisle, Cutshaw took hold of Kane's hand once more. Outside, on the steps, he turned and said simply, "I dug it." He was silent on the drive back until the car pulled up to the door of the mansion. Then he said in a childlike voice, "Thank you."

"Why did you keep the dollar?" Kane asked him.

"For suckers," said Cutshaw, and he glided into the mansion. He came out again quickly.

"If you die first and there's life after death, will you give me a sign?" he asked.

"I'll try."

"You're terrific." Cutshaw crouched away. A mist of rain began to descend. Kane looked up at the sound of distant thunder. He stepped into the mansion's main hall and met Fell, who was buckling the belt of his trench coat. "Did Cutshaw behave himself?" he asked.

"As usual," answered Kane.

"Why did you take him?"

"He wanted to go."

"Stupid question."

"Where are you going?"

"Over to the beach."

"It's cold and it's raining," Kane said.

Fell glanced at him oddly. "I'm just going there to eat, not to swim, old sport. There's a diner there with great eggs Benedict. You want some? Come on."

"No, I think I'll lie down for a while. I feel tired." Fell gave him a searching look. "Excuse me," said Kane. He walked past Fell toward the staircase.

"Sure sorry," said Fell. "I was hoping you'd come so you'd pick up the check." Kane seemed oblivious, walking on. Fell shook his head. He changed his mind about going out. He headed for the mess in search of coffee and did not notice Krebs coming out of Kane's office. The sergeant hurried after Kane.

"Colonel? Colonel Kane, sir?"

Kane stopped and turned at the head of the steps. There were heavy, dark sacs beneath his eyes. And pain. He waited for Krebs to reach him.

"Colonel?"

"What is it?"

"Well, it's just the new man, sir."

"New man?"

"The new inmate, Colonel. He got in about half an hour ago. I put him in your office. I'd thought you might not want him to be mixing with the others until you'd—well—sort of explained things to him. He seems—well—pretty straight, sir. Just combat fatigue, from the look of him. That's as much as I know."

"I'll be there in just a minute."

"Very good, sir." Krebs retreated down the stairs.

Kane entered his bedroom. He locked the door and walked into the bathroom, where he plucked an aspirin bottle from the medicine cabinet and shook its contents into his hand until he reached the 100-milligram Demerol tablets he had pilfered from the drug chest. He took three of them: nothing less could allay the pain.

He went down to his office. As he opened the door, Cutshaw approached him. "Would you please talk to Reno?" the astronaut complained to him. "Could he get his fucking dogs the hell out of the tunnels? There's slippage enough as it is down there."

"Yes, I'll tell him," said Kane. His voice was subdued.

"I want to talk about Christ's resurrection," said Cutshaw. "Do you think it was bodily?"

"We can talk about it later," said Kane.

"No, now!" Cutshaw threw open the door all the way. The new arrival, a Marine Corps lieutenant named Gilman, was sitting on the sofa, a rain-moist duffel bag at his feet. A Z-shaped scar was etched into his brow just above his right eye. He looked up at Kane, startled. "I don't believe it," said the lieutenant. " 'Killer' Kane!"

In the fall of 1967 he was in Vietnam in command of a Special Forces camp just south of the perilous demilitarized zone. Once, at the end of a particularly hazardous mission, a second lieutenant discovered him standing by a tree at the rendezvous point. He was staring vacantly into the dusk.

"Colonel Kane!" the lieutenant whispered. "It's me —Gilman!"

Kane's head was lowered. He did not answer.

Gilman squinted into the gloom. He came closer and noticed the wet blood streaking the grease paint that covered Kane's face. He followed Kane's stare to the jungle floor and saw the frail and bleeding body of a black-pajama-clad Vietcong. It had no head.

"You got a Charlie," Gilman said tonelessly.

"Just a boy." Kane's voice was dreamy. He lifted unseeing eyes to Gilman's. "He spoke to me, Gilman."

Gilman stared uneasily. Kane was partially turned away from him. "Are you all right, sir?"

"I cut off his head and he kept on talking, Gilman. He spoke to me after I killed him."

Gilman was alarmed. "Come on, sir, let's go," he urged. "It's getting light."

"He told me I loved him," Kane said dully.

"Christ, forget about it, Colonel!" Gilman's face was close to Kane's. He squeezed his arm with heavy fingers.

"He was only a boy," said Kane. Then Gilman stared in horror as Kane raised his hands. Cradled in them was the severed head of a fourteen-year-old boy. "See?"

Gilman stifled a scream. Savagely he knocked the head out of Kane's hands. It rolled down an incline and finally thumped against a tree.

"Oh, my Christ," moaned Gilman.

Eventually he got Kane back to the base. But when Kane was put to bed he was still in a trancelike state. A medical orderly recorded the incident, noting that Kane would bear further observation.

The following morning Kane behaved normally and continued with his duties. He seemed to have no recollection of the head. In the days to come he was to wonder why Lieutenant Gilman eyed him oddly whenever he saw him. Kane made sure that Gilman never again accompanied him on a mission. He could not pin down his reason for this; somehow it just seemed more efficient.

Some two weeks after the incident, Kane was standing by a window of his adjutant's sandbagged shack. He was staring at the drumming torrential rain that had not ceased for the last four days. The adjutant, a darkeyed captain named Robinson, was hovering by a TWX machine that spewed out messages a chattering inch per thrust. It mingled in ominous syncopation with the pounding of the rain.

Kane suddenly started; then relaxed. He thought he'd heard a voice from the jungle: a single cry that sounded like "Kane!" Then he saw the bird taking off from the treetops and remembered the screech of its species.

There was an unaccountable trembling in his fingers; a twitching in his bones: they had been his companions ever since first he had come to Vietnam; they and the sleeplessness. And when he slept he was haunted by dreams, chilling nightmares always forgotten. He tried to remember them but couldn't. There were even times when he would tell himself in a dream that surely this time he would remember. But he never did. Each humid morning's only legacy was sweat and the drone of mosquitoes. Yet the dreams, he knew, never left him: they still ran darkly through his bloodstream. Behind him he could sense vague tracks, feel menacing eyes that were fixed on some easy prey within him. He was nagged by a prescience of disaster.

The TWX machine clicked its teeth without pause.

"Can't you turn that damned thing off!" snapped Kane.

"Special orders coming in, sir," Robinson told him. The machine fell silent. Robinson ripped away the message. When he looked up, the colonel was gone and rain splattered in through an open door. Robinson carried the message to the doorway and saw Kane walking toward the jungle; he was coatless, hatless, instantly drenched in the violent downpour. Robinson shook his head. "Colonel Kane, sir!" he called.

Kane stopped dead, then turned around. His hands were cupped before him like a child's catching the rain, and he was looking at them.

The adjutant flourished the message. "It's for you, sir!"

Kane walked slowly back to the shack and stood staring silently at Robinson. Trickles of water plopped down from the bottoms of his trousers and sleeves and puddled on the floor.

The TWX machine had received a set of special orders assigning Kane to the state of Washington. Robinson looked rueful as he handed them to Kane. "Oh, well, Christ, it's an obvious mistake, sir. Some half-ass computer must have goofed." The adjutant pointed to some wording. "See? Your serial number's wrong, and it gives your MOS as 'Psychiatrist.' There must be another Colonel Kane."

"Yes," murmured Kane. He nodded his head. Then he took the TWX from Robinson and stared at its contents. His eyes were alive with struggle. Finally, he crumpled the TWX in his hand and went out into the rain again and walked until he disappeared from view. Robinson kept staring into the torrent. His heart was heavy. Kane's recent behavior had been anomalous. It had not gone unwatched.

Night fell suddenly. The adjutant paced in his quarters, chain-smoking nervously. Kane had been gone for hours. What should he do? Send out a patrol? He would like to avoid it if he could; avoid the necessity of explaining that "Colonel Kane took a walk in the rain without a hat, without a coat, but I thought it in keeping with his recent behavior, which has generally seemed unglued." He was protective about the colonel. Everyone else regarded Kane with a mixture of awe, dislike and fear; but he had treated Robinson gently, sometimes even with fondness, and had let him glimpse, from time to time, the sensitivity trapped within him.

Robinson crushed out a cigarette, picked up his pipe and chewed on the stem. Then he saw Kane standing drenched in the open doorway. He was smiling faintly at his adjutant. "If we could scrub away the blood, do you think we could find where we've hidden our souls?" he asked. Before Robinson could answer, Kane had walked away and down the hall to his room. The adjutant listened to his footsteps, the opening and muted closing of his door.

The following morning Kane told Robinson that in spite of the discrepancies in the orders, he thought them correct with respect to their substance. He would go to Washington.

Robinson knew he would have to report it.

"By the time he hit the States, they'd caught the mistake." Fell sat against the edge of the clinic examining table. He popped a cigarette from a packet and with shaking hands struck a match. He inhaled smoke and then blew it out. "By then it was clear that he meant to go through with it." Fell cupped the burned-out match in his hand and stared at an ad on the crumpled matchbook, a technical training school promising employment; then he slowly turned his gaze on each of the grave, bewildered faces of the men he had gathered together in the clinic: Groper, Krebs, Christian, the medical orderlies—and Gilman. "They'd heard a lot of stories about him cracking. He seemed on the edge of a very bad breakdown. When he took the assignment, though, that was it. We knew that he'd had it." Fell shook his head, and then continued. "But how do you tell a man with a record like that?"

Groper looked down at a set of orders in his hand. He shook his leonine head, amazed; then he thrust the orders out toward Fell. "These orders of yours," he said to him. "They're for real?"

Fell nodded. "You can put it in the bank," he said firmly. Then he pulled at the cigarette. "Kane didn't pick his line of work." The words came out softly, with exhaled smoke. "In World War II he was a fighter pilot. Then one time he bailed out behind enemy lines and had to fight his way back. That time he killed an even six. It happened again. And he killed five more. So headquarters figured he had a talent. And they made him a specialist. They'd drop him behind the lines on clandestine missions and let him get back as best he could. He always did. And he wasted a lot of the enemy. A lot. With a knife. With his hands. Most times with a wire. And it ripped him apart. He was good. A good man. We stuck that wire in his hands and said, 'Get 'em, boy! Get 'em for God and country! It's your duty!' But part of him didn't believe it; the good part. That's the part that pulled the plug. Then some computer dropped a stitch and gave the poor bastard a halfway out: a way to find help without facing his illness; a way to hide, to hide from himself; and a way to wash away the blood: a way to do penace for the killing—by curing.

"You see, at the start it was just a pretense," Fell continued. "But somewhere on the way back from Nam it developed into something more; much more. His hatred of the Kane who killed became denial; and in time the denial became so overwhelming that it totally obliterated Kane's self-identity: he suppressed the Kane who killed and became his better self—completely. Except when he dreamed. In the conscious state he was Kane the psychiatrist; and whatever contradicted that belief he denied and incorporated into his delusionary system."

Fell looked down at his cigarette ash; it was long. He cupped a hand beneath it and tapped it off. "Ah, my God, he had it all," he said. He shook his head. "Fugue states, redeemer complex, the migraines. You all must have seen some of that—the pain. That's what got him into drugs."

Krebs looked down at the floor as though abashed.

"Krebs knew," said Fell.

Krebs nodded, still downcast, as the others turned and looked at him. "Anyway, I talked them into letting him go through with it," Fell resumed. "It was an experiment. Partly. That was part of it. So they let him go ahead. Kane was inside the problem, looking out— an inmate functioning as a psychiatrist and coming to bear on the problem like nothing we'd ever seen. We hoped he might come up with some new insight. Oddly enough, I think he did. I think the other inmates have been responding to him. But he's suffered a setback today. A pretty bad one. Really. Bad. You see, his one big hope of a cure for himself is to wipe out his guilt by a saving act; to cure the other men, or at least see improvement. But that takes time—time and your help."

Fell gestured toward Groper. "You've seen my orders. I'm in command. But I want Colonel Kane to play out the string." Fell turned to Gilman. "Gilman, I want you to try to convince the other inmates that you were mistaken. That shouldn't be too difficult to sell around here. Can you do that, please, Gilman?

Would you do that?" A note of pleading had crept into Fell's voice.

"Oh, well, sure," said Gilman quickly. "Sure. Absolutely."

"Thank you." Fell turned to the adjutant. "Groper, you and the rest of the staff will back up Gilman. So will I."

Groper looked up from the orders, befuddled. "Colonel, let me get this straight," he said. "You've really been in charge here all the time?"

Fell nodded. "That's right," he said. "He's Vincent Kane. I'm Hudson Kane. I'm the psychiatrist. Vincent is my patient." Fell's eyes were flooding and his voice began to crack. "When we were kids I used to always make him laugh. I was a clown. And I've been trying to help him . . . remember me. But he won't."

He could not hold back the tears any longer. He said, "He's my brother."

Kane awakened in his room. He was lying on his bed, fully dressed. He sat up with an awareness of something being wrong. He saw his brother leaning forward in a chair by the bed, an odd expression of concern on his face.

"How are you feeling?"

Vincent stared without comprehension. "What? What's going on?" he asked. "What happened?"

"You fainted. Don't you remember?"

Vincent looked disturbed. He shook his head.

"What *do* you remember?"

"Nothing. I was walking to my room and now I'm here." He looked puzzled. "I fainted?"

Hudson looked at him intently. "You remember the new inmate?"

"New inmate?"

"You don't."

"What the hell are you talking about? What's going on?" He sounded angry.

Window glass shattered and a rock flew into the

113

room. It hit a wall, fell on a nightstand and bounced to the floor. Enraged and hysterical, Cutshaw called up from the mansion courtyard: "Tell me all about God, you butchering bastard! Tell me again about goodness in the world! Come on down here with your wire, you bastard! Come on down!"

The psychiatrist looked at his brother anxiously; he saw the consternation on his face. "Dumb bastard Krebs," he muttered. "He let a package from Cutshaw's mother go through without bothering to open it. I *knew* it was booze."

"Come down here!" Cutshaw shouted. "Come on down here with your wire!" Then there was sobbing and the wrenching cry: *"I needed you!"*

Vincent Kane stared numbly. The blood was beginning to drain from his face. His brother got up and moved quickly to the window. He saw Cutshaw running off. He cupped his hands and shouted after him, "Tell your mother to send you some mix!" He went back to the bed and sat by Vincent. As he took his wrist to check the pulse, he said, "That California panther piss will kill you. I heard it grew hair on a clam once. Honest."

His brother's gaze was upon him, unblinking. "He was angry," Vincent said. "That's so strange."

Outside they heard a motorcycle engine revving up. Someone shouted, "Cutshaw!" Groper. The motorcycle roared away.

Vincent Kane got up from the bed and went to the window in time to see the motorcycle break through the wooden barrier at the sentry gate. His brother came up behind him.

"He crashed through the sentry gate," said Vincent, alarmed and confused.

"Just another part of life's rich pageant."

"Why would he do that?"

"It's Saturday night."

Vincent Kane looked deeply troubled. He touched the pad of a finger to the edge of a jagged spear of glass in the window. His brother watched with tragic eyes and murmured softly, "No. No memories. No laughs."

Vincent turned with a questioning stare. He said, "What?"

"Get some rest." The psychiatrist moved toward the door. "I'll send a couple of the orderlies to pick him up."

"But they won't know where to find him."

"He can't go far." He opened the door and said, "Don't worry."

The psychiatrist stepped out into the hall. He decided he had better go and find Cutshaw himself. He would bring Gilman along and see if the astronaut accepted the change in Gilman's story. If he did not, the psychiatrist decided, he would have to risk taking Cutshaw into his confidence. He hurried down the stairs.

Vincent Kane sat down on the bed and stared at the broken glass in the window. His head was throbbing. Something was awry. Something wrong. What was wrong? He'd experienced somnambulistic lapses before. That wasn't it. What was it? Cutshaw. Cutshaw. His breathing came shallower and faster. He felt a weight in his stomach, an unfocused feeling of guilt. He stood up.

He must look for Cutshaw himself.

Cutshaw had roared through the town of Bly and come upon a seedy roadside tavern six miles beyond. There he stopped. Soaking wet, he went inside and sat at a cramped little booth at the rear. Within half an hour he was drunk. Around him, boisterous laughter drowned in the hard-rock music from a jukebox. A motorcycle gang held control of the tavern, filling it with shouts and murmured obscenities, with worn black leather jackets, the words "The Chain Gang" emblazoned on their backs. Some slouched at the bar. Some danced, matted hair and dirty fingernails jerking through the cigarette haze in the dimness of the wood-paneled room. Cutshaw did not notice. He lifted a shot glass to his lips and gulped its contents, a finger of Scotch; he grimaced and chased it with a gulp of beer, and then stared blearily at the five full shot glasses aligned on the rough wooden table in front of him. He looked up as the waitress walked by. She was young. "Hey, hold it!" Cutshaw reached out and took her hand; he could feel a simple wedding band. "How about another Scotch?" he asked slurrily.

The girl's smile brought a wholesome brightness into her face. "Sir, there's five right there in front of you," she said with good humor. Disengaging her hand, she moved on toward the bar. Cutshaw looked down at the table, disconsolate. "I wanted *six*," he murmured thickly.

Two cyclists leaning at the bar were darting glances at the astronaut. One slurped his beer and stared. His face was thick with a stubble of beard and he wore large-lensed yellow glasses. "It's him, Rob," he said. "I *know* it's him."

"You're nuts," drawled the other cyclist. He wore an open leather vest over a short-sleeved T-shirt that showed off his enormous muscular arms. He had degenerate good looks and thick blond hair pomaded into waves. Arrogance smirked out of his eyes. Stenciled on the front of his T-shirt were the words "I Love To Fuck." He was the leader of the gang. "You're seein' things, Jerry."

"Up yours. I've seen his picture in the papers."

"Since when have you ever read a paper?"

"Okay! TV!"

The waitress came up to the service bar. "Two beers, two bourbon rocks," she ordered. She glanced at the cyclists nervously. The gang was not local, and she felt a disquiet at their presence.

"Look at him!" said Jerry. "Look at his face! That's him! The astronaut! The one who lost his marbles!"

The waitress turned her head to look at Cutshaw.

"What's he doin' in a dump like this?" Rob demanded.

"Oh, who the fuck knows," Jerry answered. "But it's him. I swear it! I'm positive!"

"Yeah? For how much?"

"For a beer."

"And a blow job from either your old lady or mine." Rob was grinning.

Jerry rubbed at his chin as he glanced toward Cutshaw again. Then he downed his drink and said, "Okay."

The two cyclists wove through the crowd to Cutshaw and stood by the table looking him over. The astronaut was lifting a shot glass when he saw them. He paused, eying one and then the other.

"Yes?" he said.

"What's your name, mac?" asked Rob.

"Rumpelstiltskin."

Rob snatched the shot glass away from Cutshaw and looked sideways at Jerry. "Wise ass," he said.

As if oblivious, Cutshaw picked up another shot glass. Again the cyclist snatched it away from him, this time roughly. "I said, what's your name?" An ugly menace had crept into his voice.

"My maiden name or married?" Cutshaw looked past the two cyclists and called out, "Waitress!"

Jerry made a sudden move, pulling back a fold of Cutshaw's cardigan to disclose the initials "U.S.M.C." stitched above the chest pocket of his fatigues. He pointed in triumph. "See? U.S.M.C.—that's Marines!"

"No, no, no, my dear boy," drawled Cutshaw. "That's Unbridled Sex for the Masses Club."

Rob tossed the contents of a shot glass into Cutshaw's face.

"Is it something I've said?" asked the astronaut mildly, licking out his tongue for a taste of the Scotch.

The waitress appeared. "Yes?" she asked Cutshaw. She was frowning, puzzling over his identity. She noticed the wetness on his face and darted an apprehensive look at the cyclists.

"One Scotch and two spittoons, love," Cutshaw ordered. "Fill the spittoons with caterpillar blood. It's for our friends here. Maybe they'll—"

Jerry grabbed Cutshaw's fatigue shirt, jerked him up and forward and savagely cuffed his face.

The waitress looked alarmed. "Hey, cut that out!" she cried.

"You mean this?" Rob said to her, smirking. He quickly reached a hand beneath her dress and squeezed her buttocks. She whirled around with a cry and knocked his arm away. The cyclist grabbed her wrist and pressed his body against hers. Moaning with exaggerated, mocking eroticism, he backed her into the end of the booth divider. *"Much* better." He grinned. "Better position."

The waitress grimaced in pain and loathing. She pushed at his chest. "Oh, my God, get away!"

Cutshaw lurched to his feet. "Cut that out!" he said, moving to help her. Jerry shoved him back down in the booth so that Cutshaw's head struck against the wall. "Jesus Christ," he moaned. He was dazed.

"Move it, baby," said Rob, leering. Light gleamed from a silver cap on his tooth and he undulated forcefully back and forth.

"I'm pregnant! Get away from me!" cried out the waitress. "Stop pressing! Stop it! Please! You're hurting me!"

Jerry ripped Cutshaw's dog tag from his neck. He examined it quickly, then called to Rob: "Hey, it's him! It's really him! I got his dog tag, Rob! It's *him!"*

Rob looked over at Jerry, amazed. He reached for the dog tag. The waitress wriggled away.

"You're kidding!" Rob grunted, examining the dog tag. He looked down at Cutshaw. The astronaut was holding his head. "I can't believe it!" Rob moved a few steps to the jukebox. He pulled out the plug. In the sudden silence there were groans and complaints.

"Hey, quiet! *Quiet!"* Rob stood up on a chair. "Hey, guess what we got here! A goddam celebrity, folks! A chicken, wigged-out astronaut!" There was a mixed reaction from the crowd. Rob pointed to the booth where Cutshaw was pinned in his seat by Jerry. "That there is Captain Billy Cutshaw, gang!"

The crowd was incredulous, gleeful. A few of the cyclists applauded. One drawled, "Big fuckin' deal."

Rob stepped down and went back to the booth, where he and Jerry jerked the astronaut to his feet. "Yeah, I know," muttered Cutshaw, his eyes half closed. "Resistance is useless. My friends have confessed."

"Wanna join our club?" Rob grinned.

"Fuck you."

Rob's grin curled away to a sneer. He could not identify what he hated about the astronaut; he felt it as a pain when he breathed. He cuffed him viciously with the back of his hand and Cutshaw's head snapped back. "Okay," Cutshaw muttered. *"Don't* fuck you." Rob grabbed him by the front of his fatigues and then dragged him to the center of the room, where most of the cyclists gathered around them. One of the couples continued dancing even though there was no music.

Rob snapped his fingers at Jerry. "Beer!"

"One beer comin' up," retorted Jerry. He went to the bar to fetch it. "Beer," he told the barkeep, a man in his sixties who owned the tavern. He filled up a stein and as he set it on the bar he flicked a glance toward a telephone on a wall outside the rest rooms. Jerry followed his gaze and shook his head at the bartender. "Uh-uh," he warned him. "Don't fuck with the party." He picked up the stein and took it to Rob.

The cyclists were gathered around in a circle, murmuring, chuckling, throwing questions at Cutshaw: "Wha'dja do, lose your nerve?" "Hey, whadda they feed you in the nut house?" "Where's your keeper?" "You got any grass?" Cutshaw stood meekly, with his head bowed down. He did not answer.

Rob took the beer from Jerry. He flourished it around, and then loudly announced, "First we baptize the chicken mother!" An ugly tension, an unmotivated spite masquerading as playfulness, moved through the crowd like a malevolent sheepdog, touching them, nuzzling, herding them together. "Now I wanna hear a countdown!" shouted Rob. "Let me hear it! Ten!" he began. The cyclists joined in with him, shouting, their eyes bright as they counted down to "One!" And then Rob added "Zero!" and slowly poured the contents of the stein over Cutshaw's head. Rob grinned. He said, "Everything A-O.K. there, fuckup?"

Kane leaned his head forward, squinting to see through the rain-flooded windshield of the staff car. He had been through Bly. At each public place where he'd seen a motorcycle parked, he stopped, went inside and looked for Cutshaw. Once he thought he passed another staff car, but he could not be sure. Now he followed the road that spurted northward past the town. He had made no conscious decision to do so; the action was intuitive, automatic. A neon light was blinking ahead of him. He pulled off the road and lowered his window. It was a tavern. He saw the motorcycles parked. They were all of the chopper type, high-handled. All but one. Kane got out of the car and went into the tavern.

The cyclists were in a circle. They were singing "Fly Me to the Moon" in a slow waltz rhythm, and in time to their singing they were passing Cutshaw back and forth along the circle, shoving him, laughing, Cutshaw a limp rag doll, unresisting, unheeding, uncaring.

Kane paused at the entrance to the tavern. He stared at the cyclists. Then he caught a flashing glimpse of Cutshaw before he tripped and fell to the floor, disappearing from view.

"Get your ass up, moon boy!"

"You lookin' for rocks?"

Amid laughter, Kane slipped sidewise through the circle and quickly knelt beside the prostrate Cutshaw. Kane slipped a hand behind his back and propped him up.

"Hey, look at *this* shit," said a cyclist.

"I think we just got us another beach ball," said another one, a girl with a nasal voice.

Cutshaw stared at Kane. A purplish bruise commanded his cheekbone and blood smeared his lips from a cracked front tooth. "Been meeting your family," he said sardonically. The remark made no sense to Kane. He pulled the astronaut to his feet and began to move him toward the door, but Rob intercepted them, grabbing the astronaut's arm and squeezing. "Hey, that's my beach ball, man," he told Kane. "Put him down."

"Let him go, please," Kane said softly.

"You leggo of my beach ball."

"You tell 'im, Rob!"

"Call the M.P.s!"

"The S.P.s: that's the Shit Patrol, man. He's their leader!" Kane turned his head and looked at Cutshaw. The astronaut was staring at him, a thin, bitter smile on his face. "Here's your goodness in man," he challenged ironically; yet his voice cracked as he said it. He looked away.

The leader looked at Cutshaw in mock astonishment. "Did you say somethin'? Huh? Did you talk?" He looked at Jerry. "Jesus, Jer, I think this beach ball here just talked! I swear to Christ!" He slapped Cutshaw in the face. "Did you talk?"

"This man is ill," said Kane. "Please let us go." Rob saw the pleading in his eyes, heard the meekness, the quaver that shook Kane's voice. One of the girls said, "Let 'em go." Rob glanced at her, a blonde with pigtails, and he put his smirking face close in to Kane's. He said, "Don't say 'Please.' Say 'Pretty please.' I wanna know you mean it. Now go ahead and say it."

Kane could not fathom his own reluctance. He swallowed hard. "Pretty . . . please," he said at last, and started to walk forward with Cutshaw; but Rob kept his grip on the astronaut's arm and yanked him back.

"I'll bet he sucks," said a cyclist with a wisp of beard in the cleft between his mouth and his chin.

The leader looked suddenly inspired. "Say 'Marines all suck,'" he instructed Kane gleefully. There were giggles and hoots from the crowd. "Let 'em go," said the girl with the pigtails again. She was staring at Kane. The leader grinned at her cockily. She was his girlfriend. "Cool it, there, sugar," he told her. He returned his attention to Kane. "Come on, come on, let's get it over with; say it and you can go. Just say the words and you can split. Now whaddya say? You gonna say it? What's the harm? Then you can go." He put on a comically sincere expression.

Kane's body began to tremble slightly. He turned to

look at Cutshaw. The astronaut's gaze was on the floor. There was no expression on his face. He listened. Kane turned and fixed Rob with wide shining eyes. His mouth had fallen slightly open.

"Come on, come on—you gonna say it?"

Kane tried to move his tongue, to form words. He could not. He mounted a massive effort of will. "Marines . . . Marines . . . all . . . suck."

A sighing murmur went up from the crowd.

The girl with the pigtails moved away from the group.

"Now just one more thing," said the leader. "I swear it; this is it, then you go. Jesus, this is an easy one. Really. Just say you're a beach ball. Simple. That's it. Go ahead. 'I'm a beach ball.' "

Kane's eyes had not moved from the leader's. They were wider now, shinier. His tongue was thick and dry as he uttered, "I . . . am a beach ball."

"Just in time!" Rob crowed. "We needed a new one!" Jerry stuck his leg out in back of Kane and Rob shoved him in the chest. Kane went sprawling to the floor. The gang cheered. Rob's girlfriend watched from the bar.

Kane rose slowly to his feet and the gang began shoving him back and forth. He was passive, unresisting. He kept seeking Cutshaw with his eyes, even after the astronaut averted his face. The howling and cheering slipped the knife of headache into his skull. A plumpish girl with a mole on her chin stuck out her foot in front of Kane and tripped him. He fell down. He rose to his knees and did not move, his eyes fixed on the floor, disoriented. The leader approached him with a beer and poured most of it over his head. "Another baptism, folks. Praise the Lord." "Praise the Lord!" they shouted. "Hallelujah!" Jerry stuck a boot in Kane's back and kicked him forward. Kane's face hit the floor. Rob moved over and poured the remainder of the beer on the floor in front of Kane. His lips parted wetly in a sneer. "Fuckin' slob," he said. "Now clean up the mess!"

Kane stared up at him numbly. Jerry came over and shoved on his head until his face was almost touching a foaming puddle of beer on the floor. Rob sank down to one knee beside Kane. "Now lick it," he told him. "Lick it up." Rob's eyes were gleaming. His face gleamed excitement. "Lick and we'll let you guys go. This time I mean it."

Forgotten for the moment and dazed, Cutshaw had stumbled over to the bar. Now he turned in sudden anxiety. "Hey, knock that off!" he called out. He lurched forward, but two cyclists quickly pinned his arms.

"Lick it!"

Kane stared down at the beer. He trembled as a darkness surged through his bloodstream, a powerful secret calling his name, now in whispers, now louder, asserting, demanding. It held his tongue in place in his mouth. Kane fought it. The name. What name? He suppressed it, repelled and afraid. He opened his mouth, and his tongue slipped out in fractions, then in jerks. He licked at the beer.

An astonished sigh went up from the crowd. "Holy Christ," breathed the girl with the mole. "He did it!"

Rob smiled contemptuously, looking down. Kane drew himself up on his hands and knees and Jerry knocked him to the floor again from behind with a kick of his cleated boot. He sneered, "That's for disgracin' the fuckin' uniform."

Cutshaw struggled to free himself. "You bastards!" he cried. "You fucking sons of bitches!"

Rob walked over and cracked both sides of Cutshaw's face with a vicious hand. "Get him down," he told the men who were pinning his arms. Cutshaw was shoved to the floor on his back and the two held him down as Rob now mounted him, his crotch in close to his face. He unzippered his fly and removed his penis. He placed two fingers beneath it and flopped it up so that it touched the astronaut's lips. "Okay, fly me to the moon, now, pal," Rob leered. "One way or another, you're blastin' off!" He grinned around at the crowd, who were murmuring and giggling. A few came closer, their faces excited. Cutshaw grimaced and jerked his head aside. "If he does it, I'll be famous," Rob exulted. He drew a switchblade knife from his boot; its gleaming long blade clicked out into place. Rob held the point to Cutshaw's neck. "Come on, let's go, or I swear to Christ, I'll cut you! I mean it!"

Kane pulled himself to his hands and knees again and stared at Cutshaw and Rob. At first the scene did not register; then his eyes became separate hells. He looked up at Jerry, who was standing above him with another full stein. "I think this schmuck needs another beer," drawled Jerry. He poured it over Kane's head. He smirked at the crowd. He did not see the lip curling up, the fury. Kane reached up a hand and clasped it over the fingers that Jerry had cupped around the stein. Jerry looked around, and in a mocking, babying tone he said, "Ahhh, I think he wants some more." Suddenly his mouth flew open in a quick small gasp of horror. He tried to scream but could not as Kane's hand squeezed against his own with unthinkable force. Jerry's eyes were popping. Then at last came the scream as the stein shattered inward and Jerry's fingers were crushed bloodily into shards of glass. The scream became a wordless exhalation of air and he crumpled to the floor unconscious.

The room was stunned. "Jesus Christ!" someone murmured. Rob scrambled to his feet and faced Kane, who had risen to a crouch. Rob held the switchblade knife out to the side. For a moment he was fearful, undecided. Then the reasonable order of his universe asserted itself: a flaw in the beer stein, a fluke. He stuck the knife point-first in a wooden pillar near him, reached into his pocket, slipped out brass knuckles and put them on. Then he held out both hands from his sides, palms upward, confident, smiling, promising punishment. He swaggered toward Kane. Kane's fist drove into his stomach with a pile-driving force, and when Rob doubled over, Kane's knee shot up and broke his jaw with a crunch of bone. The girl with the pigtails let loose a hysterical, horrified scream. Then chaos. The girl with the mole pulled the knife from the pillar and a cyclist came at Kane with a tire chain. Kane side-stepped low, seized the man with the chain in a jujitsu hold, applied traction and broke his arm with a crunch, then turned as the girl came at him with the knife. He broke her wrist with a powerful chop and then raised clenched hands above his head; and as she bent and held her drooping wrist, he pounded his fists down onto her head and shattered her skull.

The other cyclists rushed at Kane.

Groper was pacing. Hudson Kane gazed out a window. They had been keeping watch in the adjutant's office ever since the psychiatrist had returned from Bly without finding Cutshaw. The time was 1:23 A.M. The telephone rang. Kane answered it as Groper abruptly stopped pacing and walked to the window: the lights of a car were shining at the sentry gate. "Here comes someone," said Groper. He went out to unlock the front door of the mansion. The psychiatrist followed him with his eyes as he talked to the highway patrolman on the phone. His face turned ashen. He listened. He looked shocked.

Outside, the staff car came to a halt by the mansion entrance. Cutshaw emerged from the driver's side and opened the door for Kane. He said softly, "We're here, sir."

Kane was staring ahead through the windshield. He did not move. Cutshaw put his head inside the car and for a moment he glanced at the gash below Kane's cheekbone. Then he looked up at the colonel's eyes.

They were fixed on some infinite pain in the distance. "We're here, sir," he said again. Kane turned his head and looked at Cutshaw, numb, unseeing; then he climbed out of the car slowly and woodenly and walked into the mansion. Groper held the door open for him. He glanced at Kane's uniform. It was torn and covered with stains. "I see you found him okay, sir," the adjutant said in what he hoped was a normal tone. Kane walked by him without a word, and took no notice of his brother standing in the clinic doorway. He moved toward the stairs like a man in trance. The psychiatrist saw Cutshaw standing next to him, watching as Kane walked up the stairs and then into his bedroom, where he closed the door. Cutshaw turned and met the psychiatrist's shattered gaze. "It's time you understood a few things," said Hudson Kane. "Come in." He motioned with his head toward the clinic, then stepped back and made room for Cutshaw to enter. He followed him inside, closed the door, and told him everything.

Cutshaw was stunned. A heaviness fell upon his heart with the weight of a sudden loss of grace.

"You can help him," the psychiatrist said.

Cutshaw nodded. His face was drained of color. He left the clinic, ascended the stairs and knocked on the door of Kane's bedroom. There was no answer. He knocked again. He thought he heard a voice from within. It was indistinct. He turned the doorknob and entered. Kane was sitting in a chair near an open window, a khaki-colored blanket drawn up to his chest. He was staring into nothingness. Cutshaw closed the door quietly. Kane did not move. Cutshaw said, "Colonel?"

There was no response.

Cutshaw moved closer. "Colonel Kane, sir?"

"I would like my cocoa now," said Kane. Again he fell silent for a time. Cutshaw waited, disturbed. Then Kane said, "I'm cold."

Cutshaw walked to the window and closed it. Cardboard had been taped over the broken pane. He looked out. The rain had stopped at last and the stars were bright.

"Where's Gilman?" he heard Kane ask him. He turned. Kane was looking at him, a puzzled look in his eyes.

"He's downstairs, sir."

"Is he all right?"

"Yes, sir. He's fine."

Cutshaw's eyes began to well up. He turned away and faced the window.

"Cutshaw."

"Yes, sir."

"Why won't you go to the moon?"

"Because I'm afraid," Cutshaw answered simply.

"Afraid?"

"That's right, sir." Cutshaw fought to control the quaver in his voice. He looked up at the sky. "See the stars? So cold? So far away? And so very lonely—oh, so lonely. All that space, just empty space and so . . . far away from home." Tears flooded down the astronaut's cheeks. "I've circled round and round this house," he said huskily, "orbit after orbit. And sometimes I'd wonder what it might be like just never to stop; just to circle alone up there . . . forever." Reflected starlight broke against the wetness in Cutshaw's eyes as the halting words sought their way from his soul. "And then what if I got there—got to the moon—and then couldn't get back? I know everyone dies; but I'm afraid to die alone—so far from home. And if God's not alive, that's really—*really* alone."

A police siren wailed. Cutshaw looked through the window and saw a flashing red light floating down the road. It stopped at the sentry gate like a beacon to warn away hope.

"Not . . . much time," said Kane. His voice was anxious; labored. "Time. No more time. But I'll show you . . . God . . . exists."

"Yes, that's right, sir." The patrol car was coming toward the mansion.

"And the others," said Kane, his eyes shining. "Maybe help. Try to cure . . . try to cure them. I don't know. No other way now. Time. No more time. Had to try . . . try . . . shock treatment."

Cutshaw did not move. Then he slowly turned for a silent, scrutinizing look at Kane. He asked, "What was that, sir?"

"Tired." Kane rested his head against the wing of the chair. "Tired," he repeated. He closed his eyes and in a soft, sleepy voice murmured, "One . . . example." And said no more.

Cutshaw kept staring at him. "What, sir?"

Kane remained silent. Cutshaw watched him for a time, then walked to the chair. Kane seemed to be asleep.

Cutshaw caught a gleam of something at his neck. He leaned over to examine it more closely and stifled a sob. Kane was wearing Cutshaw's medal.

The astronaut hurried from the room, afraid of awakening Kane with his crying. Soon after he had gone, a knife slipped out from underneath the folds of the khaki blanket and thudded to the blood-soaked section of rug beneath the chair. Dark-red blood continued to drip from a corner of the blanket.

Cutshaw walked to the landing. He looked down. Some of the inmates had awakened. They had come out of the dormitory into the hall and were murmuring, huddling in robes and pajamas. Two highway patrolmen came through the door and stood talking quietly to Groper. The adjutant looked grim and he shook his head; then, reluctantly, he led them into the clinic. Cutshaw watched as the clinic door closed. He sat down at the top of the landing. Something was wrong. What was it? Something. He glanced at the door to Kane's bedroom, frowning. When he turned back, he looked down at his feet and for a moment the substance on his shoe did not register. Then he reached down a finger and touched it. And was suddenly horrified: it was blood. "Oh, my God!" He leaped up and ran back into Kane's room.

Groper, Christian, Krebs and Hudson Kane stood together in the clinic across from the patrolmen. "Where is he?" the taller patrolman demanded.

"I can't let you have him," Kane said crisply. "I'm sorry."

"Come on, Colonel."

"You admitted yourself he was provoked."

"That's right, but—"

"No, goddammit! *He stays!"*

The patrolman was weary. "Look, we're taking him in, sir. Sorry. But we are. And if you won't produce him, we'll find him ourselves." He looked at his partner. "Come on, let's go, Frank," he said; and together they started for the door.

The psychiatrist threw his back against the door. "Listen, figure the odds," he told them coldly. "Every man in this room is a karate expert."

For a fleeting moment, Krebs looked surprised.

"Go ahead," Hudson Kane challenged the patrolmen. "You try to take him. And here's tomorrow morning's headline: 'Highway Patrol Guns Down Marines!' And just a little warning if you try me, boys: you'd better shoot to kill!"

For a moment the patrolmen looked uncertain. The taller one moved toward Kane, stopped abruptly and stared at his partner, then went to the telephone on the desk with a soft, inarticulate expression of disgust. Irritably he jerked the receiver off its cradle, then glared at Kane. "Can I use your phone?" he growled.

"Yeah, go ahead."

The patrolman had a change of mind. He hung up the phone. "Can we talk to the other one?" he asked.

"You mean Cutshaw?"

"Yeah; just let us talk to him."

"You promise no funny stuff?"

"No, sir, no funny stuff," the patrolman said somberly. "Nothing too funny about quadruple homicide."

As the group walked out of the clinic, curious inmates pressed in around them.

"What the hell's going on?" demanded Bennish.

"Why the cops?" asked Fairbanks.

"It's Fell," said Reno archly. "Five hundred parking tickets outstanding."

"There's nothing wrong," the psychiatrist told them. "Nothing. There's been a mistake. Now, where's Cutshaw?" he asked. "Have you seen him?" No one had. "Krebs, check in the dorm," he ordered. "And Christian, see if he's up there with—"

"Jesus!" Groper exclaimed. He was staring up over the psychiatrist's shoulder. Hudson Kane turned to follow his gaze and the suddenness of loss took away his breath. Cutshaw was walking out of the bedroom carrying Vincent Kane in his arms. Silent tears poured down his face. He stopped at the balustrade. "He's dead," he wept. "He's killed himself." His drowning eyes looked down and and embraced the face of the man in his arms. He shook his head. "He gave up his life."

13

The pine and spruce trees ringing the mansion flashed with the dappled wings of birds that caught the rays of the April sunset. A Marine Corps staff car entered the deserted courtyard and came to a halt in front of the building. A corporal emerged briskly from the driver's side and opened the door for his passenger. Cutshaw got out of the car. He wore Marine dress blues and the leaves of a major. It was almost three years after Kane's death.

Cutshaw breathed deeply and then looked around. The air was sweet. When he glanced at the courtyard a tenderness warmed his face and memories flooded him, whispering voices, echoing, fading. For a moment he closed his eyes. "Simon says . . . Simon says . . ." The corporal watched him, wondering, puzzled, as Cutshaw shook his head, with a rueful little smile. Then he opened his eyes and gently instructed the corporal, "Wait here." Cutshaw walked up to the mansion's front door. He found it locked. The corporal watched him walking around and testing windows. One was open and Cutshaw climbed inside, disappearing from view.

Within a month of Kane's death, the center had been deactivated. Twelve of the inmates were reassigned to other hospitals and clinics as Project Freud was pronounced abandoned; but the rest of those at Center Eighteen seemed suddenly restored to relative normality. As to whether they had simply put aside pretense, or indeed been jolted back to health by the shock of Kane's death, no one cared to speculate, not even Hudson Kane, who suspected that the Hamlet theory of their illness was probably correct. Yet with one exception—Cutshaw—the psychiatrist wrote up reports that certified each of the men who had returned to normal functioning as "hopelessly incapacitated for future military service" and recommended their general discharge "with honor." He would not have these men sent back into combat. For Vincent's sake.

Cutshaw looked around at the vacant main hall. It had not been restored. Great holes still gaped in the plaster walls, and the ceiling was just as Gomez had left it. A warm, sad smile came to Cutshaw's face. When he looked at the stairs winding up to the landing, his eyes grew melancholy and grave. For several moments he did not move; then he walked to the stairs and climbed slowly to the second floor. At the landing he hesitated, then continued to Kane's bedroom door and stopped. He removed his cap and for a time stood silently in front of the door, his head bowed. Then a sudden impulse urged him to knock. And he did, very softly and gently, four times. He opened the door and stepped into the room. He stood just beyond the doorway for a moment, remembering, feeling, drinking in. His gaze caught the window and he walked to the place where the chair had been. He looked down for the stain from the puddled blood that had flowed from the great, deep wound in Kane's stomach. But he saw nothing there. A death had been covered with floor wax and buffed.

Cutshaw felt in his pocket for a crumpled envelope.

He took it out. His name was written on the front. Groper had found it atop a bureau in the room on the morning after Kane's death. The astronaut reached inside the envelope and removed the letter from Kane. He unfolded it gently. It was written on notebook paper; the thin blue lines had almost faded away. The astronaut wondered again at the firmness of the hand that had produced the bold, neat writing, the graceful script which had the flourish of an invitation to a wedding.

"To Captain Cutshaw," the letter began. "I have given some thought to one of your problems, the one wherein you question why God does not end man's honest confusion concerning what it is that he expects him to do, by simply appearing to him and telling him in an unequivocal way. What if a man in shining garments appeared tomorrow hovering in the air above a great city and declared to all that he was sent to us by God; and that as a credential of his claim he would perform any miracle that was asked of him? And suppose that he was asked to make the sun do figure eights in the sky for precisely twenty-six minutes, beginning at noon on the following day. And suppose that he accomplished that. Would we believe him? Well, I think that for a while all would believe, all those who saw what he had done. But after a week or so, I fear only those of good will would still believe; all the others would be talking of autosuggestion, mass hysteria, mass hypnosis, coincidence, unknown forces and the like. It is not what we see in the sky that helps; it is what is in the heart: a right hope, a good will. I hope this helps you," the letter read. Then it went on in an everyday tone: "I am taking my life in the hope that my death may provide a shock that has curative value. In any case, you now have your one example. If ever I have injured you, I am sorry. I have been fond of you. I know someday I will see you again."

He had signed the letter, "Vincent Kane."

Cutshaw looked up and out the window. A russet glow had set fire to the sky and bathed the wood in lambent glory. Cutshaw stared with awe and wonder.

Cutshaw was on his way to the mansion's front entrance when his eye caught the door to Kane's old office. For a moment he hesitated; then he walked to the office, put his hand on the knob and threw the door open with such force that it banged against the wall and shook down plaster from the ceiling. He stared at where the desk had been and said softly, "May I go?"

The corporal was leaning against the car when he heard the crash from within the mansion. He leaped to alertness. Cutshaw walked out the front door and closed it behind him. He came to the car and then turned for one last look. The corporal followed his stare. "Sure heard some stories about this place, sir," he said. "Some psychiatrist they had here—a killer."

Cutshaw looked into the man's eyes and said, "He was a lamb."

He got into the car. As they passed the old sentry gate, the corporal cleared his throat. "If you don't mind talking about it, sir . . ." he began. "I guess everyone asks you this. . . ."

Cutshaw met his gaze in the rear-view mirror "What?" he prompted gently.

"Well, what's it really like being up there on the moon, sir? I mean, how does it feel?"

For a moment Cutshaw did not answer. Then he glanced out the side window and smiled. "That depends on who's with you," he said. The he sighed, removed his cap, put his head back on the seat and closed his eyes. He was soon asleep.

Fairbanks had returned to live with his parents in Plainville, Kansas, where he helped to run his father's granary business and then took it over when his father died several months later. He settled in peacefully to look after his widowed mother and his two younger sisters, aged ten and thirteen. He would sit on his porch and read the news from Vietnam.

Reno, whose family was very wealthy, went back to New York and attempted an acting career without success. Then he took up "serious figure skating" every day in the Central Park rink. While skating one day, he met a young nurse who worked in the cancer ward at Fordham Hospital. "This is like *Portrait of Jenny*," he told her. "Don't grow up or we're doomed." She laughed and they dated and after a reticent courtship they married. Reno's parents strongly objected: the girl, Maria, was Puerto Rican, a spawn of the slums. Reno was working on a play and they lived on her salary; his parents would not help. As it happened, Maria spent much of her salary on gifts for the patients in the ward: all of them were children, and of destitute parents. Reno thought it wonderful that she did so. One day Reno's mother caught sight of Reno and Maria scavenging the sidewalks for cigarette butts, which they would cannibalize and use to roll their own. She had just come out of Bergdorf Goodman, and pretended not to see them. But after that his parents began to help.

Fromme merely drifted for a time, sleeping late while his wife, a Las Vegas casino cashier, provided their sole support, except for Fromme's disability check. In the night he would awaken from sleep with a shout, unable to remember what it was that had frightened him in his dreams. His wife divorced him and married an air-conditioning salesman. Fromme was now working as a dealer at one of the major casinos on the strip. He was often criticized for being too friendly with the players.

One year after their discharge, both Nammack and Gomez attempted to reenlist but were rejected. Now Nammack tended bar on the island of Maui in Hawaii. Gomez had returned to civilian life to find that his fiancée had married. On the night of his rejection for reenlistment, Gomez became extremely and belligerently drunk and shot the former girlfriend's husband on the doorstep of their home with his service .45. He was presently awaiting trial.

Bennish was director of public relations for a university in Los Angeles and was living quietly in the

San Fernando Valley with a wife and one child, who was very precocious.

Krebs returned to the neurology staff of Sepulveda Veterans Hospital, where he had worked for several years until his assignment at the center. Christian married and left the corps. Groper had requested a combat assignment. It was granted. On the tenth of November, 1969, he was killed in action. He had deliberately thrown himself on top of a live grenade to prevent it from killing two young privates who were standing near it in a state of shock. He received the Congressional Medal of Honor, which was given to his mother in Pulaski, New York. She put it in a box with Groper's letters.

ABOUT THE AUTHOR

WILLIAM PETER BLATTY was born in New York in
1928 and is a graduate of Georgetown University.
After taking an M. A. in English literature at George
Washington University, he served as an editor with
the U. S. Information Agency in Lebanon and was
Policy Branch Chief of the U.S. Air Force Psy-
chological Warfare Division in Washington, D.C.
He is best known for his incredibly successful book,
The Exorcist (which has sold over eleven million
copies in Bantam paperback.) Mr. Blatty has written
several novels and screenplays, including *A Shot in
the Dark*. Currently, he and his wife Linda and their
two children divide their time between California and
Washington, D.C.

RELAX!
SIT DOWN
and Catch Up On Your Reading!